Praise for

Jenny Torres Sanchez's debut novel

THE DOWNSIDE OF BEING CHARLIE

"A unique and moving story that will connect with teens."
—*VOYA*

"Peppered with sardonic humor."—*Publishers Weekly*

"Refreshing to have a book focusing on a young man's struggle with weight and body issues." —*School Library Journal*

"Sanchez has talent for bringing a very serious issue to light in a way that teens can understand."
—Seventeen.com book club

"A strong, well-written book that takes a different perspective on a high school student's senior year."—*Children's Literature*

"Fans of Chris Crutcher, Sarah Dessen, and John Green will appreciate *The Downside of Being Charlie*. Highly recommended."
—TeenLibrariansToolbox.com

"Raw, heartfelt, searingly honest. If this is Sanchez's debut novel, this is an author to watch."—Catherine Ryan Hyde, *New York Times* bestselling author of *Pay It Forward*

"Both heartbreaking and hopeful."
—David Yoo, author of *The Detention Club*

"Strikes a delicate and heartfelt balance of honesty and wit."
—Jennifer Castle, author of *The Beginning of After*

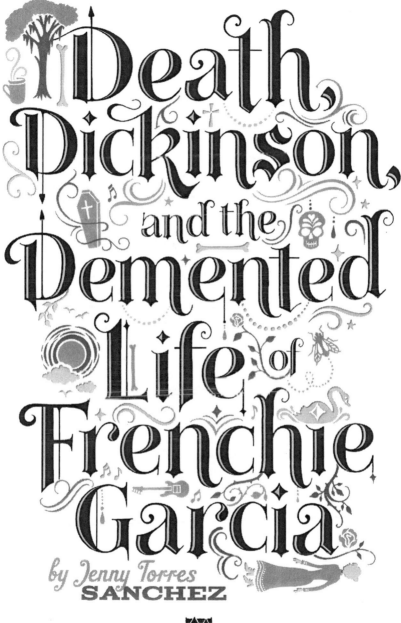

Death, Dickinson, and the Demented Life of Frenchie Garcia

by Jenny Torres SANCHEZ

RP | TEENS
PHILADELPHIA · LONDON

Books published by Running Press are available at special discounts for
bulk purchases in the United States by corporations, institutions, and other
organizations. For more information, please contact the Special Markets
Department at the Perseus Books Group, 2300 Chestnut Street, Suite 200,
Philadelphia, PA 19103, or call (800) 810-4145, ext. 5000, or e-mail
special.markets@perseusbooks.com.

ISBN 978-0-7624-4680-3
Library of Congress Control Number: 2013934992

E-book ISBN 978-0-7624-4841-8

Designed by Frances J. Soo Ping Chow
Cover illustration by Kate Forrester
Edited by Marlo Scrimizzi
Typography: Acknowledgement, HT Gelateria,
Letter Gothic, Requiem, Samantha, and Trixie

Published by Running Press Teens
An Imprint of Running Press Book Publishers
A Member of the Perseus Books Group
2300 Chestnut Street
Philadelphia, PA 19103–4371

Visit us on the web!
www.runningpress.com/rpkids

TO AVA AND MATEO,
the baby bird that died on our back porch,
& LUNA

There's been a Death, in the Opposite House,
As lately as Today—
I know it, by the numb look
Such Houses have—alway—

The Neighbors rustle in and out—
The Doctor—drives away—
A Window opens like a Pod—
Abrupt—mechanically

Somebody flings a Mattress out—
The Children hurry by—
They wonder if it died—on that—
I used to—when a Boy—

The Minister—goes stiffly in—
As if the House were His—
And He owned all the Mourners—now—
And little Boys—besides—

And then the Milliner—and the Man
Of the Appalling Trade—
To take the measure of the House—

There'll be that Dark Parade—

Of Tassels—and of Coaches—soon—
It's easy as a Sign—
The Intuition of the News—
In just a Country Town—

EMILY DICKINSON, POEM 389, C. 1862

PART 1

BECAUSE I COULD NOT NOT STOP FOR DEATH—

Chapter 1

The old man across the street is dead. I don't know who figured it out or how, but I think he'd been dead for days when they found him. School has been out for three weeks. I estimate that would have been the last time I saw him. Alive.

First the police came, and then the county coroner. We watched, Mom and I and our neighbors who never really talked to the old man, as they wheeled his body away in a black body bag atop a gurney. The world stood still as they drove him away. And then, as if someone hit play, it resumed.

People on our block trickled back into their houses, and Mom went back into ours. But I sat on our stoop, thinking about the old man. And I haven't been able to stop thinking about him since he was taken away four days ago.

I guess death is funny. Not "haha" funny, but more like screw-with-your-head funny. It makes you think strange things. Like how a person can sort of exist but not at the same time.

I imagine the old man arriving in front of a blinding light, staring at it with his milky eyes and scowling. And still another part of me imagines him safe inside his house, at his kitchen table, drinking coffee maybe. But the logical part of my brain tells me the truth, that he's either at the funeral home, or being loaded into a hearse, or already in the hearse on his way to the cemetery at the end of our block.

Living here I should be used to death. But every time a procession goes by, I wonder about the person inside the hearse. Did they live happily but die horribly? Or maybe they lived horribly but died happily? Or worse, maybe they lived horribly and died horribly.

I look at the old man's house and try to decide if it looks numb.

Moments later, his procession passes by slowly. I'm struck with indecision about what to do. If I wore hats, I'd take mine off and bow my head. But I don't wear hats. Or maybe if I stood up and gave a military salute. But both seem wrong. So I just stare. I stare at the hearse and each and every person in the string of cars that trail behind it. This is my great show of respect. But I can't help it. I can't help but wonder how they're all connected. If any of them feel guilty. If any, even, are to blame.

When the last car passes, I consider following it and joining the throng of mourners dressed in black. But crashing a funeral can never be good. I look down at my black Converse, thinking about the old man who went by Kinsky/Keniski/Kenesky or something like that. I wonder why even though I didn't know him, he makes me want to cry.

"Hey!"

I blink back tears and look over to see my best friend, Joel. His dreads are pulled back so they aren't hanging in his face the way they usually do. He comes over and puts one heavy black boot on the step I'm sitting on.

"Hey," I say. "You're back." Joel lives with his dad but visits his mom and stepdad in Chicago the first couple of weeks of every summer. He usually calls me while he's there. Usually we've already made plans for what we're going to do the day he gets back. Usually. But he hadn't called me the whole time he'd been gone or in the three days he'd been back. So I pretend like I couldn't care less that he's here.

"I'm back," he says and sits down next to me. "Did you miss me?"

"Yeah, I barely got out of bed." I hope the remark sounds sarcastic enough to cover up the truth of it. I pretty much did nothing but sit around, watch TV, and eat Cap'n Crunch for breakfast, lunch, and dinner the entire time he was gone. I don't exactly live a glamorous life.

"How was Chicago?" I offer.

He shrugs. "Not bad." Joel actually hates going to Chicago because he despises his stepdad. That's why he lives with his dad here, even though his dad is kind of weird and maybe even a little scary.

"Did you scope out some apartments?" I ask him. We had been planning to move to Chicago since our freshman year in high school, and even though I hadn't been accepted to the art school there, we were still planning to hit Chi-Town until I could reapply.

Joel looks toward the cemetery. "Some. But slim pickings."

"Oh," I say, disappointed. I had kind of wished Joel would come back and tell me he found a place so we could get the hell out of here next week. "Well, we better figure it out soon. That's why I kept calling you . . . ."

He nods. "Yeah, sorry. My mom had all these things she wanted to do, and you know how it is," he says.

"Right," I say.

He looks toward the cemetery and says, "So, anybody die while I was gone?"

I point to the house across the street. "The old guy."

"Oh, damn," Joel says this the way people do when death hits close but not close enough to hurt. "That sucks," he says. He takes off his sunglasses, hangs them on the collar of his torn up vintage Ramones T-shirt I gave him last year for his birthday, and stares at the old man's house. After a while he says, "Let's go to Harold's."

We head down the street in the opposite direction of the cemetery. As we turn onto the main street, I shake my head at the sign I pass every day on the corner leading to the cemetery. Dead End. That's the kind of humor death can have.

As we walk, Joel takes out two cigarettes and hands me one. He lights it for me and I inhale as he tells me about his trip to Chicago. I try to pay attention, but the heat and stickiness of another Florida summer is making me irritable and the bright sun gives me a headache. I wipe away the sweat beads forming above my lip and on my forehead.

This heat is pretty bad when you're sitting still, but absolutely unbearable once you do something as crazy as move. I'm convinced the Southern drawl came about because even talking was too strenuous in pre-air-conditioning days. God help them. As the sun beats down on my head I seriously consider shaving off all my jet black hair or maybe even bleaching it so it doesn't absorb so much of the punishing heat.

I look over at Joel. "I don't know how you can walk around with that hair. It's like permanently wearing a dirty wool hat." I give Joel lots of grief about his dreads, but actually, I love them. And he knows it.

He grins. "Please. They rock and you know it. And what

about you? Your hair in your face like that all the time," he says and gestures to the messy look I usually go for.

"I know, it's just so freaking hot," I whine. My legs feel heavier with each step I take and I feel like I'm slowly melting. In the distance, I see actual heat waves, making the street look warped and distorted.

"We should've driven there. Why didn't we drive?" I say.

"It's only like four or five streets away," Joel says, taking another drag from his cigarette. "Don't you care about our environment? Like your carbon footprint or some shit like that." He flicks his cigarette butt on the ground.

I fan myself with my hand, which blows weak little puffs of hot air on to my face before realizing that moving my hand like this makes me sweat more.

"One or two streets in this humid inferno is more than enough reason to hop into your ride and join the millions who contribute to global warming every day," I tell Joel.

He shrugs and keeps walking. The heat makes my thoughts drift back to the old man. I wonder if he's in the ground yet. What happens to a dead body in this kind of heat? I try to count the cracks on the sidewalk and take the last drag of my cigarette. I try to remember what makes heat waves. But my mind is already thinking about a corpse, under all that dirt, in this raging sun.

"God," I say.

"What's wrong?" Joel asks.

"Nothing, it's just so damn hot."

We get to Harold's House of Coffee and Tea, which is a little hole-in-the-wall café hidden in a residential neighborhood in downtown Orlando. Most people don't even know it's there unless they live around here because it's a two-story house that was converted into a coffee shop. The café is on the lower level and Harold and his wife live on the upper level—very old school and very cool. Joel opens the door, and a gust of cold, heavenly air swoops out and greets us. It immediately revives me. I love AC.

"If I ever have a kid, I'm going to name it AC," I tell Joel.

"Right," he says.

"What? I'm totally serious. AC, or maybe Freon."

He shakes his head. "French, no offense, but I can't exactly see you with a kid someday."

I think about that for a minute. "Okay, you're right. Maybe I'll name my dog Freon."

"You hate dogs."

"My fish?"

"Sure, your fish," he says, "who you'll kill right after you get him."

I shrug. "Fair enough."

Joel and I order some iced coffees and then sit down in our usual spot—a big green couch in the corner.

"So," he says, looking at me the way people do when there's obviously something that needs to be discussed but nobody wants to say it. I look at him expectantly.

"So," I say.

"So . . . I'm really sorry I blew you off the last few days. Lily had some stuff planned when I got back. I'll make it up to you, though."

"Whatever," I say, even though it was more than a few days. See, Joel is in serious like with this girl Lily. He met her about four months ago at a local punk show. Now the world basically revolves around her and Joel has little time for anything, or anyone else.

But like I said, whatever.

"No, really," Joel says. "I know it was kind of crappy of me."

It was more than kind of crappy. But had I really expected any different?

"Where is Lily anyway?" I ask, because if he's here, then she must be busy.

"Band practice," he says. "Which reminds me, Sugar is playing at Zylos tonight. You in?"

Sugar is the name of Lily's band. Of course, because that's

exactly the kind of name someone like Lily would name it. I take a big gulp of my iced coffee.

"Hold on, let me get this straight. You totally ignore me for the past two weeks and now you want to hang out with me at your girlfriend's show?"

"Come on," he begs, "I said I'll make it up to you. How about a movie? We can go see the one about the orphaned zombie girl. You've been dying to see it, right?"

I'm surprised he remembers.

"My treat . . . ," he says.

"Fine, I'm in," I tell him, even though I don't want to be in. And the idea of getting ready and going to a show just to pretend I like somebody is too much effort. But I am kind of glad he's back. And maybe the thrill of Lily has died down a little and things can go back to how they used to be.

"Cool," he says and smiles. The way he smiles reminds me that Joel and I have been close since middle school. There's not much we wouldn't do for each other, and so I almost ask him. I almost ask him to ditch Lily tonight so we can hang out. So we can go to the movies tonight instead of some other night and talk about the cool parts afterward as we eat really bad food at some crappy all-night diner. And maybe that will help me stop thinking about dead people.

But you always think about dead people, Joel says in the imaginary conversation we're having in my head.

I know, but now I can't stop.

And a zombie flick is going to help this? he asks.

Maybe not, I agree, *but maybe it would at least make me feel like things were normal again.*

Okay, he says.

Great, I say.

And I watch us leave.

But that's not the conversation we have. I tune back to our real convo, which not surprisingly, is much more one-sided than the imagined one in my head.

"I Skyped with Lily so that made it not so bad," he says.

I sigh. "That's cool."

"And I bought her a Wrigley Field keychain because she's never been to a baseball game in her whole life. Can you believe that? How can someone go their whole life without going to at least one baseball game?" Joel says.

"It happens," I say.

I'm tired of hearing about Lily and try to think of something new to talk about. "So, I saw them wheel out the old man," I say.

"Really?" He pauses for a minute, then says, "That sucks."

I nod. It did in fact suck. But worse, what I just said brings forth the image of another body, on another block, being wheeled out of his house in another bag. And now I can't say anything more. And the conversation turns back to Lily.

I mutter the obligatory "that's cool" at appropriate times before tuning him out again. I picture myself at home, on the couch, with a bowl of cereal while I watch crappy daytime TV.

After awhile, the buzz of Joel's meaningless chatter finally stops and I guess he takes the hint that my apparent disinterest stems from genuine disinterest. So he suggests we go and we head out.

"Call Robyn and tell her to come tonight," he says, referring to our unofficial third best friend. I feel like telling him to call her himself, but instead I say I will, since it requires less energy.

I turn in the direction to my house, but not before I watch him head in the opposite direction toward his house.

As I watch him leave, I can't help but feel deflated. And alone.

Chapter 2

"**I** feel like shit," I tell Emily Dickinson.

She's the best person to talk to when I feel this way and she's a good listener. But maybe dead poets usually are.

It isn't *the* Emily Dickinson. That one is buried at a family cemetery in Amherst, Massachusetts. But I discovered this grave here during my freshman year and always thought it was pretty incredible. And even though she's not the famous poet, I pretend that she is. I imagine her right there, six feet under, in a white lace dress, eyes closed, and listening to me; the hermit dressed in white who didn't come out of her house for years, whom the children were afraid of. I feel oddly connected to her. I think we would have been great pals if, you know, she weren't dead and I had been born a couple of hundred years ago.

Em and I also shoot the shit sometimes. It's easier than dealing with the kind of drama that comes from talking to live people. I call her Em for short and she calls me Frenchie, short for Francesca. I know you think she probably doesn't like being called Em since she looks like one of those uptight Puritan types and all, but I don't really buy into that. Em had some pretty wild thoughts.

I plop down in the shaded spot under the tree next to her grave.

Here's what people don't know about cemeteries: They're a strangely comforting place. Sure it's sad, but there's also something else here—a kind of peace and refuge that you can't find anywhere else. Here, you can hide from the world for a while. Here, nobody approaches you for anything. You can spend hours here and you'll be left alone because people respect the fact that anyone in a cemetery, whether dead or alive, should be left alone. Not even time exists here, or it at least seems to stand still. It's generous. It doesn't urge you on. It lets you be.

"Joel's back," I tell Em. "And he's still Lily-crazed. We just hung out, and I was hoping maybe it would help me feel better. But nothing feels the same anymore." I sigh, disgusted with myself for actually missing school. At least then my days were filled with something.

Em keeps silent. She doesn't talk much. But if I sit here long enough, one of her poems usually pops into my head and I figure it's some kind of message.

I look over to the newer part of the cemetery. I always tell myself I'm not going to, but I do. This time I tell myself I'm just looking for the old man's gravesite. But like always, my eyes focus on someone else's.

Heart! We will forget him!
You and I—tonight!
You may forget the warmth he gave—
I will forget the light!

"Stop. I don't even care," I tell Em. Both of us know this is a lie. Both of us pretend it's not.

"Were you afraid of being buried alive?" I ask her, trying to change the subject. I don't expect an answer, so I go on. "I was . . . am. I even told Joel to hold a mirror under my nose when I die, or stab me in the heart, anything, just to make sure I'm dead."

Em nods. I suppose to her it doesn't sound so far-fetched. Joel had laughed at me and said I was crazy. Maybe if I'd never watched that medical show about a woman who was declared dead and was stuck in some cooler with a tag around her toe, and then she suddenly started breathing again, I would have laughed at the idea also. But she'd actually been declared dead. For two hours. All I could think was, what if . . . what if when she woke up, she'd already been put in a coffin and couldn't talk or open her eyes? Or what if she was already in the ground? What then?

Joel promised, but he was laughing when he did. So I made him promise again. And again. Until he wasn't laughing. I wanted him to understand I meant it, because even though the embalming fluid they pump into you would probably kill you first, what if it didn't? What if you end up down there, under all that dirt, clawing at the inside of a coffin and trying to get out?

I know I won't be buried alive. Some part of me knows that. And I know Andy wasn't buried alive. But sometimes, I can't get that picture out of my mind.

"I'll see you later," I tell Em and head back home. When I get there, I crawl into bed and try to sleep some hours away.

Chapter 3

"**W**here the hell have you been?" Robyn yells at me as she gets in my car. Her long blond hair, usually worn loose and wild, is secured in two elaborate braids on either side of her head. Being so petite, this makes her look slightly like an alien, but in a cool way. "I was getting ready to hitch a ride. You said ten thirty!"

The reason Robyn is Joel's and my unofficial third best friend is because she's a bit of a free spirit and usually off doing her own thing. Luckily, tonight she decided to do our thing and I won't have to hang out by myself all night while Joel is once again preoccupied with Lily and likely to forget me.

"Sorry, I fell asleep," I tell her. Which is true. But I don't tell her that I woke up hours ago, that I've been in bed trying to figure out a believable way to bail out of this. Or that it took great effort to convince myself to get ready and drive to her house.

She looks me up and down. "Well, I see you at least put in a little effort," she says as she opens the visor and applies more of her signature berry-berry lipstick.

"Uh, thanks?" I say.

"No, seriously. I love when you do that smoky eye makeup. It looks so good with your dark eyes. And I mean, no offense, but you've kind of been looking like a scab lately."

"And you mean no offense by that, right?"

Robyn puts away her lipstick, then turns back and studies me thoughtfully. "You know what I think you need, Frenchie? You need a guy."

"What?" I ask.

"A guy. You seriously need one."

"God, Robyn." I shake my head. "I cannot even believe you said that! Don't tell me you think that a guy is like, the solution to a girl's problems. That's so . . . I don't even know . . . man, Robyn." If I didn't know her better, if I'd just met her tonight and she said something like that, I would seriously push her out of my car.

"Oh, for fuck's sake. Relax, French. Of course I don't think that! Give me some credit. It's just that in your particular case, I think maybe some . . . how do I put this?" she says while focusing in on me. "I think you need someone to thaw out that cold little heart that's barely beating inside your chest. You need someone who warms you up, French, that gets you hot."

"You're disgusting, you know that? Seriously, please stop," I say and start wondering if I could reach over and open the passenger door.

"I know you've always been a bit rough around the edges. And I suppose you could say that's part of your charm. But lately you're even more . . . ," she says and makes a face. "I don't know. . . ."

"What?" I say. She shakes her head like she's not going there. "Come on, go ahead. Just say it," I tell her.

She taps her lips and searches for the right word. "You seem even more . . . dreary, warped, tragic. . . ."

"Tragic?"

"Cold . . . prudish . . . uninviting . . ."

For someone who couldn't find the right words, Robyn is suddenly spouting them out quite easily.

"Bitchy . . . snarky . . . evil . . ."

"Okay, enough!" I yell.

Robyn laughs. "Oh fine. Lighten up. But you see what I mean? You need to have fun. And guys? Guys can be lots of fun, French." She grins, because if anybody knows how to have fun with guys, it's Robyn.

"I am not tragic. Or evil," I tell her.

"Come on, French, when was the last time you actually fell for someone?"

When Robyn says this, I realize how people can forget. Because if Robyn really thought about it, she would remember that the last time I absolutely fell for someone was in ninth grade. That I fell and kind of stayed fallen all through ninth, tenth, eleventh, and twelfth grade for the same guy. That at the start of every year, I would search each one of my classes for a glimpse of what would make that class worth going to.

Not that Robyn is some kind of horrible, insensitive person. Despite her seemingly brash personality, she actually has a good heart. And in all honesty, I had only mentioned Andy Cooper a handful of times to her, and that was probably three and a half years ago. And it was more of a "Oh yeah, he's a cool guy" than a "this guy makes me forget to breathe" kind of mention. I didn't tell Robyn because I didn't want to admit I had unwillingly become the girl who was so hung up on a guy that she would never have the chance of getting. Or that the kind of day I had usually depended on whether or not I fulfilled my quota of Andy sightings. Because, you know, that would be kind of . . . tragic.

"You're not giving me any credit," I say to Robyn. "What about Trey Sumpter? At the end of ninth grade, remember?" Not that Trey and I exactly dated. It was more like we exchanged notes for two weeks before summer. And then when we came back to school, I saw him kissing Trisha Clove.

"That was like three years ago," Robyn says. "And did you

guys even actually talk?" I pretend her question doesn't register because she's right. I'm not sure Trey and I actually did talk. Maybe we never went out. Or worse, maybe we're still going out.

"What about Simon Kurts?" I say, but immediately regret bringing him up. Now that I think of it, nothing exactly happened there either.

"You hooked up with Simon Kurts?" Robyn asks. I think back to how Simon called me almost every night in the eleventh grade, only to ignore me at school the next day.

"I guess not. I mean, I don't know," I tell her. I'm confused and this conversation with Robyn has only made it painfully obvious that I'm hopeless when it comes to guys. I guess this is why I don't know what the whole thing with Andy meant. And now I never will.

I look over at Robyn. "The guys at our school were jerks," I say.

"The guys at our school were scared of you," she says.

The car is filled with silence, except for the steady sound of my turn signal as we wait at a stop light.

"You freak guys the hell out, French. The only one you ever talk to is Joel, and I have no idea how he managed to get on your good side."

It wasn't that remarkable actually. Joel had been the new kid who walked into my eighth-grade math class wearing a Vinyls concert T-shirt back when nobody else knew who the Vinyls were. The shirt and his moody disposition (which I later learned was because it was the year his parents split) had been the beginning of our friendship. But we quickly became best friends and soon he was spending more time at my house than his own.

"But other than him," Robyn continues "you think all other high school males are so intellectually challenged. You don't even give them a chance. And you snarl. I've seen you snarl at guys."

"That's stupid," I say as I make a right turn.

"It's true. You *need* to lighten up a bit. You're in serious need of some kind of intervention. Gloom intervention." She nods like she's confirming a diagnosis.

"There's nothing wrong with me. I'm good."

She looks at me doubtfully.

"I'm good, okay?" I try to smile to make my point.

"Is that supposed to be a smile? You look like you're in pain."

"Just drop it," I tell her.

Robyn rolls her eyes and sighs. I think I baffle her. Which is understandable. Seeing as I baffle myself.

Chapter 4

Zylos is located downtown, and it's one of a handful of clubs that make up Orlando's "nightlife." Lots of local bands perform here, but we didn't start coming here until a few months ago when Robyn met Colin, the official ID checker guy at the door.

She saunters over to Colin so he'll let us in without having to wait in line. And while Robyn, with her gypsyesque appearance of a thousand jangling bangles and flowy skirts may weird out some people, she has a certain charm that makes guys fall all over themselves to give her what she wants.

"Hey, there," she says to Colin. He's sitting on a ripped up barstool at the entrance of Zylos and he flashes a warm smile at us.

"Nice to see you back here again," he says and looks at me. I shrug and look away. He must think that checking IDs makes him irresistibly cool, probably because the girls who come here usually flirt back. I guess some girls buy into the whole dark-haired version of James Dean, right down to the slicked-back hair and cuffed jeans. But to me it just seems a bit assholish.

"So what's the story?" Robyn says to Colin.

"Same old, same old," he says, chewing on a piece of gum and checking the ID of some guy with a huge lip ring. Colin puts a pink wristband on Lip Guy's arm, and turns back to Robyn.

She props her arm on Colin's shoulder and whispers something in his ear. He laughs and leans in to murmur something back.

"Well, that's interesting," she says, looking over at me. She smiles and winks before turning and whispering back. I suddenly feel naked, especially when Colin looks at me and raises his eyebrows. His light brown eyes glimmer with amusement.

"Oh, really?" he asks Robyn.

"Good as done," she says and slaps his back. He grins and holds out a couple of pink bands for us. "Here you go, then," he says. At first I'm totally floored and stand there like an idiot since he's never done this before, but Robyn holds out her wrist without missing a beat.

He turns to me and wraps a band around my wrist. "Don't get into any trouble," he whispers. His breath smells sweet and minty from the gum. "At least, not without me." I give him a dirty look, but this just makes him laugh as Robyn grabs my arm and pulls me into the club.

"Gross," I say to Robyn once we're inside. "What did you tell him?"

"Just that you'd sleep with him," she yells back. "And maybe a couple of other things. Man, this rocks!" she says, holding up her wrist.

"Damn it, Robyn! What is your problem?"

"What? He's cute," she says.

"I don't care! Now he probably thinks he's awesome or that I would actually . . ." But she's not listening to me anymore so I just say, "Forget it. Just so we're clear, pimping me out is pretty much unacceptable. And, I'm not interested."

Robyn shrugs me off and takes in the place. It's crowded and loud and the heart-jerking beat of the music is pulsing through my body. I can feel it in my throat, in my teeth, and it's exactly what I should love. But tonight it just seems loud, monotonous, and grating.

Robyn shouts in my ear, "Let's get a drink!" We head to the bar and Robyn yells at the bartender, "Suprise me!" He smiles and grabs a few bottles that he flips and tosses around. He pours faster than I can keep up with and makes two blue drinks that he sets down in front of us. Robyn takes out some money.

"Ladies drink free!" he yells.

"And now I officially love you!" she yells to the bartender. He winks at her and I predict we're in trouble because Robyn is . . . well, Robyn. I grab my drink and take a sip that burns my throat and makes me cough, but Robyn takes a huge gulp.

We head outside to where the stage is and I spot Joel right away.

"Hey!" he calls out to us. Lily is with him and smiles when she spots us. Robyn and I head in their direction carrying our drinks.

"So glad you guys came!" Lily says and hugs Robyn and then me. I cringe when she does. It's just that some people, like me, don't like to be squeezed, touched, stood too close to, breathed on, etc. But Lily on the other hand, is a hugger and personal space invader.

"Hi, Lily," I say.

"I can't believe all these people came out for this show. It makes me nervous," she confides and looks at the growing crowd spilling out onto the patio.

"Babe, don't worry. You'll be fine," Joel says, grabbing her by the waist and pulling her into him.

I restrain from looking away in disgust.

"You guys will be great," I force myself to say.

She smiles. "Thanks, Frenchie. You're sweet to say so."

Sweet. Something that nobody has ever accused me of before.

"I just hope we don't have an off night and totally suck," she says. Lily has the slightest hint of a Southern accent. The kind that makes you think she's this sweet hometown girl and you almost forget she's standing there in a purple off-the-shoulder top, red patent-leather pants that look as if they've been painted on, and sleek platinum blond hair.

Some guy with headphones and a black Zylos T-shirt comes up to her and says, "You ready?"

Lily nods and Joel gives her a kiss. Then she turns to Robyn and me and says, "Okay guys, see you after the show!" She leaves and jumps up onstage and starts talking to her bandmates.

When she's gone, Joel turns to Robyn and me and says, "I don't know why she gets like that before a show. I mean, she's always great."

"Yeah. Great," I say.

"All right, everybody!" Lily yells into the microphone, showing no trace of the nervousness she displayed just moments ago. "You guys ready for some Sugar?"

The crowd responds with hoots and hollers. "I said, are you guys ready?" Even louder hoots and hollers fill the air, followed by a few people yelling her name. She looks over at the lead guitarist and gives a nod. He lets loose a wicked chord. The band breaks out into full-fledged hectic playing as Lily starts dancing and the crowd goes wild. Then she opens her mouth and starts singing.

And here is the cherry on top of the sundae that is Lily. She's good. Like someday, she will definitely make it big it's-just-a-matter-of-time good.

I look over at Robyn who grabs my blue drink from my hand and chugs it down. "Come on, Frenchie!" she yells as she starts dancing. "Have some fun!"

I try to get into the music and enjoy myself, but I can't. I feel stiff and out of sync. I trudge on, and pretend I'm having a great time, but I'm pretty sure I look like some kind of demented girl version of Frankenstein's monster. The band goes right from the first song to the second. And nobody misses a beat. Except me.

The second song is even better. The catchy drumbeat at the beginning pumps up the crowd even more. A bony elbow catches me right in the ribs and I lose my footing. I bump into some big brute of a guy who steps on my foot with his big steel-toe boot. I shove him hard, but he doesn't even notice. I bite my lip, and try to ignore the throbbing that's starting in my toe. More people crowd in around me as the lights onstage flash and swirl faster. I feel like I can barely breathe.

I start pushing people out of my way and force my way out of the mob. By the time I get to the doors to the main room, I have a strange sense of not really being here. A fleeting worry that maybe I was trampled on the dance floor and I'm now having an out-of-body experience runs through my mind. I glance over to see if Joel or Robyn noticed that I left, but Joel is too enthralled by Lily, and Robyn is too busy dancing to care.

The main room is now less crowded because most people are outside listening to Sugar. I make my way over to a wall and lean up against it, trying to pull myself together.

"Having fun?" I look over to find Colin next to me. "You're seriously going to have to tone it down or I'll have to throw you out," he says and laughs.

This is probably where a normal girl might giggle and say something profound like, "Haha, yeah . . ."

But I don't. I just ignore him and keep looking out at the small crowd of people who have opted out of Sugar and are dancing to the music here instead.

"Ahh, the strong, silent type I see," he says. He doesn't leave, but instead leans up against the wall next to me and watches the crowd also. I have nothing to say, but he's not leaving.

"So why aren't you out back listening to the band?" he asks.

I shrug.

"I guess it is pretty crowded out there. I prefer more quiet places myself," he says. He turns to look at me, and just then "I Don't Mind" by the Blurs comes on. I lean my head back and try to focus on the song. It's one that most people like because it sounds good, but they never stop to listen to the words, which are beautiful and quite poetic. People sing them, but without realizing their meaning.

"This is one of my favorites," Colin says. I can hear him singing along and try to tune him out.

"Are you okay?" he asks. "You seem bummed. Did you just break up with your boyfriend or something?"

I sigh and just shake my head.

He nudges his shoulder into mine, trying to be playful, I think.

"The whole love-at-first-sight thing seems overdone and all, but it seems original in this song. Don't you think?" he says. "I guess I believe in that kind of love, to some extent. You?"

I look over at him to see if he seriously thinks I'm going to fall for this crap. I may not know much about guys, but I'm pretty sure that anytime one asks you if you believe in love at first sight, he's probably some kind of weirdo you should avoid.

"Nope," I say. "But I believe in assholes at first sight."

He stares at me with an expression I can't quite read, and for a short moment, I feel triumphant. He says nothing for a while. And then the room starts feeling small and stifled. I can feel myself getting flushed and hot as he looks at me, trying to figure me out. I'm relieved when he finally turns his attention back to the people on the dance floor.

"Wow. Assholes at first sight," he says with a laugh that

makes me feel foolish. I wish I could just walk away now, but my body won't comply and I stay there, like I'm Velcroed to the wall.

"That's pretty genius," he says, smiling. "You should put that on a T-shirt or something. Sell them for ten dollars each."

"Listen," I say, "I really just want to be alone right now."

He acts as if he's mulling this over. Like he's giving careful consideration to what I've just said.

I try again. "I think I just need to leave," I tell him. "Could you make sure Robyn gets a ride from Joel? Can you just tell her I had to go?"

"Uh, yeah, sure . . . ," Colin says, the bemused look on his face replaced with confusion.

"Thanks," I say as I start walking away. "Just make sure she has a ride, okay? Please," I call out to him. "And tell her . . ." I try to come up with a plausible excuse, but Robyn will know it's a lie. "Just tell her I'm sorry."

"Okay," he yells back since I'm already far away, but not fast enough. As soon as I step outside I'm practically running to my car. I try not to think of the strange expression on Colin's face as I left.

When I get in my car I light a cigarette. I'm surprised my hands are trembling a little. I take a long drag and open the windows as I pull out of the parking lot, feeling only slightly more relaxed. The streets are dark and deserted and the air rushing in as I drive is warm and humid. And while I try not to think of him at all, I can't help it. This night. This drive. All of this.

It reminds me of Andy.

Chapter 5

"Get up, Loser!" Robyn's incessant voice booms. She jumps on my bed and I flop up and down. "Get up, get up, get up, get up! Why are you still in bed?"

I groan and resist the urge to grab her ankle and send her flying onto the floor. "Leave me alone!" I yell, pulling my blanket over my head.

She leaps off the bed, and for a moment in my half-conscious stupor, I think she might actually leave. But of course, she doesn't.

"Shitty trick you pulled on me last night! Have you ever heard of date rape, huh? Roofies? What if he'd taken me to some deserted place and killed me?"

I sit up in bed, rubbing my eyes. "What are you talking about?"

"I couldn't find Joel after the show, or at least I think I couldn't find him. You might say I went on a bit of a blue drink frenzy." She shakes her head as if clearing it. "Anyway, I ended up getting a ride home with Colin."

I rub my forehead. "Oh," I say. Realizing she's talking about last night, which already feels like ages ago. "Uh, so what's the big deal. I thought you knew him."

"Well, I do. But I don't know him, know him."

"Wait," I say, "But didn't you try setting me up with him?"

"Oh yeah." She laughs. "But like that'll happen now, hearing as you were your usual charming self."

"What?"

"He told me all about it. That you believe in assholes at first sight?" Robyn says and goes to my window. She pulls on the string that opens my shades and lets an ungodly amount of light in.

"Close those!"

"You really are a child of darkness," she says. "Now get ready. We're going to Harold's. Joel and I have been calling you for the past hour." I reach for my phone. No charge.

"How'd you get here anyway?" I ask Robyn since I'm basically her unofficial taxi driver.

"Um, hello, I have legs," she says gesturing to them as if I had any doubt.

"You walked?" I say in shock.

"God, French, you're really slow in the morning. Now come on, get up. You're going to Harold's. You owe me at least that much."

"Fine," I say and reluctantly roll out of bed and go brush my teeth. When I come back I see Robyn pulling clothes out of my closet. "What are you doing?" I ask her.

"Aren't you going to change?" she asks.

I shrug, but change from the T-shirt and jeans I fell asleep in last night to the fresher T-shirt and jeans that I find on my floor.

"Let's go," I say.

We get to Harold's and after ordering the usual, I sit on the couch and wait for Robyn while her drink is being made.

I take a sip of my iced coffee and stare out the large glass windows in front of the shop.

Across the street, a young boy with a Goofy shirt runs down the steps of a house and pulls at the locked door of a car. His parents, both with sunglasses on and water bottles in hand, stand at the front door and talk to someone in pajamas in the doorway.

Tourists. On their way to Disney no doubt. Their gleaming white socks and tennis shoes are almost as blinding as the stucco walls of the house from which they just emerged.

I watch as they continue talking to Pajama Lady. They say their farewells before finally unlocking the car with a *beep, beep* for the poor kid who's still pulling at the handle.

I pity them because here's the thing nobody says in

brochures: Florida isn't so much the Sunshine State as it is a crematorium. And as you walk down Disney World's Main Street, as you melt and the soles of your shoes stick to the asphalt, you and ten thousand other visitors will walk aimlessly about in a heat-induced hallucinatory state, wondering how something so wonderful, so promising, could be so absolutely fucking miserable. But you slap on a happy face because "It's a Small World" plays somewhere and makes you buy into that happiness. And if you can't be happy here, then where can you be happy?

The family drives away. I'm about to turn my attention when I notice a guy walking his dog along the sidewalk in front of the house. The dog stops and does his business on Pajama Lady's lawn. And then the owner looks around and tugs at its leash without picking up the mess.

And here's what I picture happening later on today: The kid will step in it. He'll probably come home, unaware of the misery that is a theme park in the dead of summer, still believing in a safe, fake little world. He'll rush up to tell Aunt Pajama Lady all about it and as he relays the thrill of the vertigo-inducing rides, they'll all smell it.

And they'll all see how it's been tracked into the house and onto the beige-colored carpet. As they all figure out he's the culprit, he'll feel terrible. And when he thinks about it ten years from now, the memory of make-believe lands, he'll always remember how he stepped in shit and ruined his aunt's carpet.

When I look away, I've been staring at the blinding light so long, all I see are black dots as Robyn plops down on one of the oversized beanbags. I try to focus on her.

"So, what the hell?" Robyn asks, expecting some kind of answer to this vague question. "About last night?" she reminds me.

"What about it?"

"Um, hello, why'd you bail?"

"I just wasn't in the mood for more Sugar. I'm on Sugar detox," I say.

"You could've gotten me. I would've left, too," she says.

"Well, you didn't exactly look like you wanted to leave," I say as I rub at my eyes and Robyn's face comes into more focus.

"Okay, you're right," she says. "But it looks like I've finally got something going on with Bobby." Bobby is Sugar's drummer, and Robyn has been after him ever since we first saw Sugar play. "Did you see the way he looked at me last night? He looked good."

"Doesn't he have a girlfriend?"

"Not anymore," she says, and smiles in a way that lets me know she likely had something to do with that.

"You're terrible," I say.

"I know." She grins, but then her attention is suddenly drawn to the door and she gets the crazy-eyed look that alerts me to

Robyn's no-good schemes.

"Okay, French, don't lose your shit. And remember how much you love me."

"What?" I ask, following Robyn's gaze and turning around just in time to see Joel, Lily, and Colin walk in.

"Why is Colin here?" I ask Robyn, who is now waving madly at everyone and completely ignoring me. I meet Colin's eyes for a second, but then avoid any further eye contact with him. Now that we're away from the darkness and reverberating music of Zylos, I'm slightly ashamed of my behavior last night.

Joel smiles at us. "Hey, guys," he says, walking over.

Lily hugs Robyn and despite my refusal to get up from the couch, she manages to somehow hug me while I'm sitting down.

"Hey, French," she says as she squeezes me.

"Hey," I say weakly. As she pulls away I look down and unintentionally notice her toes peeking out of her open-toed shoes. Her toenails have this cutesy red-and-pink-striped design on them with sparkles.

"Oh, wow. Uh . . . nice toes," I say more to myself, but she overhears.

"Oh, thanks," she says and smiles. "It's super easy. You could totally do it." I force a smile.

Lily looks around Harold's and sighs. "I love this place," she says. "There's such a cool vibe here."

"Right," I say. I shift my attention to the newspapers and magazines sprawled out on the coffee table next to me and I start to reorganize them. As I do this, Colin comes over and sits next to me—a little too closely. I move my leg away so we're not touching.

"Hey there," he says. "I got your girl here home last night."

"Oh, yeah, I heard. You're a hero," I say without thinking.

"I'll take that as a thank you?" he says.

Joel and Lily go to order their drinks but Colin stays where he is.

I make eye contact with Robyn and scowl at her, but she just plays dumb and shrugs her shoulders. She and Colin exchange a brief but meaningful look, and then he kind of clears his throat and looks down at the floor. I suddenly get the feeling they know something I don't. I grab one of the newspapers off the pile I've just organized and open up to the obituaries.

"Dexter Mavree died yesterday at the age of eighty-one. He is survived by his three children," I read aloud. I scan the rest of it. "Look, they used an exclamation point in his obituary. Doesn't that seem wrong? I mean, shouldn't there be a rule against using exclamation points in obituaries?" I ask.

There's a moment of silent awkwardness before Colin coughs and announces that he's going to get some coffee. He leaves and I turn to Robyn.

"What the hell is going on? Why are you still trying to set me up?" I hiss.

"Please, Frenchie. You barely stood a chance after last night. And now, with your insightful and demented reflections on punctuation and death, well, let's just say I don't think I'll have to hold the guy back. I mean, seriously?" She looks at me and shakes her head.

I don't respond.

"Okay, listen. So, first stop this crazy bullshit." She rips the obituaries out of my hands, which makes a loud tearing sound and leaves me holding a tiny strip of paper. Colin, Lily, and Joel look over at us. I can feel my face getting red. Robyn waves at them and offers a little smile before leaning closer to me. "Second, here's what I'm thinking, you just need a boost, a little nudge is all, to get out of this funk. Go have some fun. Go be wild. Act like a normal person. Look," she demands, "Colin is cute and he digs you, French. Despite your doomish and off-putting ways, he thinks you're cool."

"He doesn't even know me. How can he think I'm cool?"

"We talked about you last night," she says. Oh God. I can only imagine what Robyn told this guy, especially if she was sloshed on those blue drinks. "That despite your odd behavior, you really are a cool girl . . . when you're not on your period."

"You told him I was on my period? Robyn!"

"Come on, don't be so close-minded, French. What's the big deal?"

I look over at Colin who is leaning against the counter. He smiles and kind of waves when he notices me looking at him.

"It's not like you gotta marry him. Look, you're down because you and Joel used to hang out all the time and now there's Lily. I get it." The words hurt more than I thought they would. "And you guys had plans to move to Chicago before you got rejected from art school. . . ." Damn, was Robyn trying to make me feel better or worse? "But, you need to stop moping around like this. Life goes on."

I'm kind of speechless. I mean, feeling like a loser is one thing. Being told you're a loser is another.

"Have," I say, finally. "We *have* plans to move to Chicago. That's not changing."

Robyn looks at me. "Right. But until then"—she says and cocks her head in Colin's direction—"I'm just saying."

Colin is heading back with his coffee, followed by Joel and Lily. Robyn leans back on the couch as if her work here is done.

Lily sits next to me, and Joel sits on the armrest next to her. Colin looks around, and finally settles for a beanbag chair on the floor across from Robyn.

Everyone keeps praising Lily about how fantastic she was last night. She's all modest and shit, which irks me because, please, like she doesn't know she's good? Does she have to be convinced of it?

And then everyone asks her all these questions about her music and stuff. You'd think Lily was getting interviewed by *Rolling Stone*. I mean, I don't care what bands inspire Sugar or how they identify with the garage band/postpunk movement.... It all just seems so nonsensical and unimportant. After another five minutes, I can't take it any more.

"Sorry," I say, "But I have to go. I've got stuff to do," I say.

"Again? Come on, what could be better than hanging out with us?" Joel asks.

Giving blood, having surgery, passing a kidney stone . . .

"Just . . . stuff, okay?" I say. Joel's eyebrows go up. I realize my response might have come across a little more like an outburst.

"Fine, go," Joel says.

I stand there a minute because everyone is looking at me.

"Okay, then. I'll see you guys later," I say. I push open the door, aware that they're all sitting there, quietly watching me go. I squint at the bright sun as I exit Harold's, and once again head out into the hot, little, hellish inferno that is Florida. I have the lingering feeling that they all must think I'm a bit of a psycho. I almost care. Except I don't.

Chapter 6

That night at dinner, my parents are watching me.

"What?" I ask them.

"What? Nothing," my mom says.

My dad shakes his head and shrugs his shoulders. "Nothing."

"You guys are staring at me," I say.

Mom laughs. "What? We can't look at you now?"

I sigh. There's been some tension in my house lately, and it all comes down to art school. See, my parents are real artsy kinds of people, not overly parental, but hell-bent on creativity and this notion of raising "a capable, independent individual who will contribute to society." And since my mom is an artist and my dad is a musician of sorts (he has an office job but a room full of guitars he still plays), they hope my contribution will be an artistic one. It's kind of like they want me to save the world, using art. No pressure or anything.

My mom's been planning my future as an artist from the moment she saw how long I could sit with a sketchbook in front of me. And most of this year, she'd urged me to finish the sample pieces I need for the application. And I did. She urged me to get my letters of recommendation. And I did. She reminded me to make sure I submitted everything before the deadline, which I also did. And everything should have worked out great. Except I didn't get in. And it's been the big giant elephant in the room ever since.

"I was just wondering," my mom says, peering around the elephant's ass, "if you've been working on anything new lately?"

They look at me, like quizzical birds, waiting for their little bird to say something.

"Uh, no," I say. I stare at my chicken and suddenly feel sorry for it. I push it around on my plate, trying to ignore the echos of a cluck.

"Oh," Mom says. She takes a few more bites, chews, swallows, and then speaks up again. "You should," she says. She does this in a singsongy way meant to sound like she's not nagging. "Maybe it would be good for you. It might inspire you a little. Especially if you're going to reapply."

"Um, yeah . . . ," I say. I don't bother to tell her that I don't care about getting into art school anymore. I keep staring at the chicken.

Mom puts down her fork, which is always a bad sign. It means she's so into whatever she's about to say next, that she can't be bothered with operating a utensil at the same time. "Frenchie," she says.

I put down my fork, too unable to eat any more of the chicken and push away my plate. I decide I'm a vegetarian from now on.

"Frenchie," Mom says again and waits until I look up. Her face softens. "It's not the end of the world," she says.

I close my eyes and rub my forehead. "I know, Mom," I tell her.

"There's always a second chance. There's always next time."

Except when there isn't. There's not always a second chance. I nod.

"Your mom is right," Dad says as he cuts his chicken. The knife scrapes the plate, and then he pops the piece into his mouth. I feel sick.

Mom gets up and walks over to her purse. She pulls out her wallet.

"Here," she says, handing me a credit card. "Please, just go to the supply store and get some things. You'll see. Once you smell the oil of the paint and turpentine and pencils, once you see the blank canvas, you'll get inspired."

"Mom." I groan because I really don't want to go. How can I explain to her that I already tried. That I've been to the art supply store several times. And every time I walk in, the smell makes me panic. The blank canvas makes me anxious. The weight of everything in that store closes in on me and makes me never want to pick up a paintbrush again.

"French, just go," she says. The softness in her voice from a moment ago is gone and replaced with a stern tone. I know this tone. It means she's lost her patience with me.

"Fine," I say, because I don't have the energy to sit here and argue with her. She stands there, holding the credit card.

"What?" I ask. "You mean now?"

"Right now."

I look over at Dad who just shrugs, but then says, "You'd better go," in a way that means he's siding with Mom.

I push back my chair and grab the card from Mom's hand. "This is so stupid," I say.

"I'll be anxious to see what you get," she says. I give her a dirty look and grab my keys off the counter.

"And Frenchie," she calls as I open the front door. "Remember, we love you."

I slam the door extra hard, no doubt leaving them to discuss all the possibilities for what is basically just a bleak and uncertain future.

I curse myself for not pulling a Van Gogh by cutting off an ear, wrapping it in a fake acceptance letter, and presenting it to my parents.

I have the distinct feeling it would have been less painful than what I face now—forcing something that I just don't have.

Chapter 7

I start driving. But instead of going to the art supply store, I speed to the end of my block and come to an abrupt stop in front of the cemetery. I get out of my car and cross through the familiar gates. For a moment, I actually consider going over to Andy. I want to. But I can't. Instead I cut over to Em's grave, reciting some old familiar lines to the beat of my steps.

I felt a Funeral, in my Brain,
And Mourners to and fro
Kept treading—treading—till it seemed
That Sense was breaking through—

And when they all were seated,
A Service, like a Drum—
Kept beating—beating—till I thought
My Mind was going numb—

And when I heard them lift a Box
And creak across my Soul
With those same Boots of Lead, again,
Then Space—began to toll,

As all the Heavens were a Bell,
And Being, but an Ear,
And I, and Silence, some strange Race
Wrecked, solitary, here—

This poem I've memorized. There's nobody around to hear me, and I find comfort in the way Em's poems sound. They do this kind of halting thing at the end of some lines. It's like you expect them to rhyme, to keep going smooth and seamless, but they don't. And in a weird way they do . . . in an awkward kind of way. Slant rhyme bothers the shit out of some people, but I like it. If I were a poem, I'd probably be in slant.

I look at Em's grave.

"You get it," I tell her, because she's the only one who does. I see the world going on around me, but I'm stuck. And the monotony of every day is like that steady drum, just beating, beating, beating, while each day passes.

"I feel that steady beat in my head, Em. I march through my days like those mourners, but I feel like I'm in that box, too. There's a funeral in *my* brain. How do I make it stop?"

But she doesn't have any suggestions so I say the poem again, consoled only by the fact that she understands me. Maybe because she completely cut herself off from the rest of the world. I wish I could do the same. I wish I could go in my room and never be bothered again.

I hear the last lines echo with the steady march.

Wrecked, solitary, here.

There's something sad but immensely appealing about it.

I look across the cemetery and notice that Mr. Nice Old Man is here, in the newer part of the cemetery. Nice Old Man is a nice old man who has been coming to the cemetery every weekend for the last year. He's always dressed in a suit and bow tie and brings a fresh rose to put on the grave of a woman named Rose Griver. I think it was his wife. He only ever stays ten minutes and I guess that's because conversations with the dead can be incredibly one-sided. It makes me sad when I see him reach for his handkerchief and hold it to his eyes. Even more sad when I see him leave, heading down the curving, twisting roads that lead out of the cemetery. Sometimes this place seems like a labyrinth trying to confuse the living so as to keep them here. I think of Nice Old Man alone in his house, without Rose.

A rose for Rose.

I smile remembering Faulkner's short story we read in class last year, "A Rose for Emily." Even though it's kind of sick . . . and sad, and the Emily in the story is a recluse and kind of demented, I love it.

I look back at Em's grave. "Did you ever read 'A Rose for Emily'?" I ask her. Em shakes her head no, so I proceed to tell her about it. As I'm telling her about the main character in the story, I start to wonder if Faulkner wrote the story because of Emily Dickinson. Maybe he pitied this great poet, so he offered her a rose in the form of a story.

I see Emily's lips purse up in annoyance at this thought, but I can't help it. I connect the dots from the Emily in Faulkner's story in her dreary black dress and gloomy house, to Emily Dickinson in her ghostly white dress peering out the windows of her Amherst house.

And then I see myself tucked away in my house down the street from a cemetery.

Am I warped and doomed? It's a ridiculous thought because I'm really nothing like the Emily in the story. I mean, I would never kill a guy and hide him in my attic.

Although, maybe, in a way, I did kill a guy.

I look over at Andy's grave. For a moment, a horrid moment, I imagine myself digging him up, taking his skeleton, and then locking it up in my room. It scares me, the way that thought came out of nowhere. So I quickly transport Andy back to his grave and pack the dirt over him again.

"What's wrong with me?" I ask Em. But she's still miffed by my comparison of her and Faulkner's Emily. I pity Faulkner who is about to get an earful.

I figure I better get some kind of art supply thing to pacify my mom, but I can't bring myself to go to the art store. So I say farewell to Em and drive to Super Target instead.

I watch people as they walk around, how they look at clothes, buy DVDs, and drink giant red slushies from the in-store café. There are moms buying diapers and tween girls looking at nail polish, trying to pick between neon green or electric blue. There are six cashiers scanning countless things people buy, listening to countless beeps. Like that older lady with too blond hair. Her shifts are probably about six hours long, with a thirty-minute break in between, which means five and a half hours of *beep, beep, beep*. She could die on her way home tonight, and her last moments were spent ringing up this other lady's cotton balls and Crock-Pot. Or the lady purchasing them could die instead and she'll have spent her last moments trying to decide between this Crock-Pot or that one. How many hours or days or years do we spend doing useless things, making unimportant decisions, thinking about things that don't matter. And is that what life is? Just a series of unimportant things that in the end don't matter?

I grab some Cap'n Crunch because I refuse to waste time deciding on any other kind of cereal, and pick up a pack of crayons and markers. Maybe I can convince Mom that I'm returning to a time when art made me happy.

Chapter 8

A week after meeting them at Harold's, I haven't talked to or hung out with Joel or Robyn at all. It's normal to go this long with Robyn, but not really with Joel. Or maybe now it is. The weird thing is, I don't know if I care. I wonder if it's possible he forgot I existed. The more I think about it, the more I'm convinced it's plausible. Maybe I imagined our entire friendship. Maybe Joel has always wondered why I hang around him so much and he never told me to get lost because he feels sorry for me. Maybe in the end, we are all just nobody to each other.

I'm Nobody! Who are you?
Are you—Nobody—Too?

"Here," Mom says, interrupting my thoughts and handing me another red poppy that she's planting in the garden. She insisted I help her.

At least they're not roses.

It's Saturday and a procession comes by while Mom and I are on our knees digging up dirt. I look away and refuse to look inside the cars that trail behind the hearse. I watch Mom instead, as she brushes the dirt from her gloves. She doesn't quite watch, but she stops digging for a moment.

"Life is strange," she says when the last car has made it past our house. "It is, then it isn't. Just like these flowers." She sighs and deposits the last plant into the hole she's dug, then pats the earth around it.

"Well, that's it," she says.

I get up and take a look at the front garden. It seems ironic to me, how we can bury these little flowers, and they sprout with life.

Mom goes inside to get us some drinks and I wonder about the person who just went by. I wonder what his or her obituary said. I make a mental note of the date to see if I can search for it later.

I've actually tried to write my own obituary, but it's hard. Not because imagining myself dead is heartbreaking, but probably because the idea of it is much different than the reality of it.

All my accomplishments thus far have been physiological. All I've really managed to do is stay alive for seventeen years, and really, that's mostly due to my parents. They're the ones who make sure I don't get eaten by a wild animal or something. So all

I've accomplished is managing to breathe in and out for seventeen years, which doesn't even require conscious thought.

Francesca "Frenchie" Garcia breathed in and out for seventeen years.

That's all I've ever come up with.

I've pictured my funeral more than once. Lots of times, actually. I don't know why I do that either. I think Mom would put flowers in my hair, maybe ones like these red poppies. I think of the mourners, the quiet, the procession, and the formal black. If it weren't so terrible, a funeral could almost be beautiful. If you let yourself forget that the eyes are sewn shut, that the skin is cold, that they're putting someone in a hole forever to never see light again, it could almost be lovely.

Mom comes out with the drinks and I almost ask her what she would include in my obituary, but decide not to because she'd wonder why I think such things. And I don't have a good answer for that. So we sit quietly and drink lemonade.

"You think that person was old?" I don't quite realize I've said anything until Mom answers.

"Yeah," she says quickly. But then she hesitates and looks down the street. "I sure hope so."

That night I have trouble sleeping. I dream the same dream about Andy, the one where he's my prom date.

I'm wearing horrendous layers of pink taffeta as he leads me out to the middle of the dance floor. But instead of dancing, we lie down and the floor opens up beneath us, and suddenly, we're in this big hole. Mom and Dad and Joel and Robyn appear above us, talking to each other while looking down at me, but I can't hear anything they're saying. Then a priest appears, which doesn't make sense because I'm not even Catholic, and a disco ball keeps twirling high above that reflects red and gold lights everywhere. I try to tell everyone I'm not dead, but my lips feel sewn shut and my arms and legs are stiff and heavy and impossible to move. And even though my eyes are wide open, they start throwing dirt on top of me. Right when I almost can't see anything anymore, Andy's mom appears above me, dressed in black. She peers in and asks, "Is that her? Is her name Frenchie?"

This is where I always wake up. Right when Andy's mom makes eye contact with me. Right when I see the sudden realization in her face that, yes, I am Frenchie.

Chapter 9

The following morning/afternoon, I lie in bed trying to think of a reason to get up. But I can't think of one, so I just stay in my room.

A few years ago, I decided to make my room look like a painting I'd seen of Van Gogh's bedroom. The first time I saw it, I was immediately struck with how the layout was identical to that of my room, down to where the window and bed were positioned. So naturally, my first thought was that I was Van Gogh in a past life. Of course I then realized the utter ridiculousness of such a thought. But in some egotistical way, I guess a part of me hasn't really let go of the notion, which is why I went to all the trouble of painting my walls that same shade of blue, as best I could match it, and setting up most of my furniture as true to the painting as possible. And my room became one of my favorite places to be, rivaled only by the cemetery.

Andy had liked Van Gogh. My junior year I sat diagonally from him in English class. One day, as he sat sideways in his seat, like he always did before class started, I came into class and slammed my Van Gogh sketchbook on my desk. Andy had said, "Van Gogh," and tapped his black pen on the cover.

"Yeah," I'd said.

"Cool guy."

"Well, I don't know him, but I hear he was pretty great," I answered, even as my stomach flipped with excitement at having something in common with Andy Cooper.

Andy had smiled. "Kind of crazy," he'd said, pulling on his own ear. He knew about Van Gogh's ear. I was impressed.

"I like crazy," I told him.

He looked down at the floor, and then he looked back up at me, his hair falling over his eyes, making my hand tingle with an impulsive desire to reach over and touch it.

"I'm crazy," he whispered.

My stomach drops and a little bit of acid creeps up into my throat as I remember those words.

I'm crazy. That's what he said. I should have asked him what he meant.

But I didn't. Instead, I acted like I was in a straitjacket and said, "The voices, Mommy, the voices!"

Andy cracked up and I still remember the warm feeling that washed over me when he pointed at me with his pen and said, "Funny."

Andy Cooper.

He was exactly the kind of guy I swore I'd never like. Exactly the kind of guy I'd make fun of for looking a little too pretty. Verging on preppy. The kind of guy who would vacation with his family somewhere like Martha's Vineyard. Definitely not the kind of guy I'd run into at a club checking out a local band.

But there was something about the way he carried himself, something about the way he looked disinterested in everyone, not because he was arrogant, just because he was preoccupied with something in his thoughts, that always made Andy the kind of guy you wanted to know. Whose thoughts you wanted to read. The kind of guy who you somehow knew was more than what he seemed.

And that year, when I sat near him, I realized I was right. Andy Cooper was cool. And a little bit of a paradox. I mean, sure he wore khaki shorts and boat shoes without socks, and looked like he might be a conceited prick, but the boy read poetry and liked Van Gogh. He carried a book of poems with him all year, and in class discussions, he always said some pretty deep stuff that made me forgive his prettiness.

Most times when I saw him in the halls, he was by himself. But the weird thing is Andy was incredibly popular. I think everyone wanted to figure him out, or maybe everyone thought they had him figured out. Maybe that was the problem. Either way, I think everyone felt weirdly drawn to him even though he was never really close to anybody in particular. People knew him, but they didn't really know him. Only if you watched him day in and day out for a few years, did you realize Andy wasn't at all who you would think he was. I feel like only I knew that. And maybe Zeena Fuller, who was the only girl Andy ever dated that I knew of.

I close my eyes. I see Andy glancing back at me saying, "I'm crazy." Did he really say that?

I run through the memory again, trying to recall everything exactly as it happened. But the harder I try to remember, the more unsure I am of what he said, until I'm left wondering if that moment even happened at all.

The doorbell rings, cutting into my thoughts, and I listen as Mom answers the front door. I hear a tone of surprise in her voice as she talks to whoever it is, and then the door shuts with a thud and footsteps get louder as someone comes down the hallway to my room. I look at my clock. Noon.

There's a knock on my partially open door. "French?" It's Joel. A small surge of annoyance shoots through me.

"Come in," I say, but he doesn't. "I said come in."

"I have to make an entrance," he says from the other side.

I sit up and look at the door.

"Are you ready?" he calls.

"Yeah, I guess. But what do you mean?" The door opens slowly, and then I see him and nearly die.

"Well?" Joel says. "What do you think?"

"What the hell, Joel!" I think he's gone mad. I think I'm going to cry.

"It was Lily's idea; she's the one who did it, actually. But I was so ready for it," he says.

Of course it was Lily's idea. Who else would advise Joel to shave off his dreads.

He rubs his hand through his now nonexistent hair as he comes in my room. He sits down on the edge of my bed and all I can do is stare. It doesn't even look like Joel anymore.

"It's crazy, huh?" he says with a grin. And then looks at me like he's waiting for an answer.

I close my mouth. Open it again. Then close it and swallow the lump in my throat.

"Well?" he demands, "Say something."

"It's so . . . different."

"Different? Oh man, French. Why don't you just tell me I look like shit?"

"No, no, you look good. It's just . . . different. You look so . . ."

"Dashing?" He laughs again, and I swear, it's like I haven't seen him this peppy in a long time, and that's saying a lot since he's been so freaking happy lately anyway. He almost seems . . . lighter.

"Lily loves it. But I gotta admit, I kind of freaked out when she suggested it last night, but then I thought it really is time." He looks around my room. "I'm kind of ready for something new, you know? I mean, think about it. This is probably the one time in our lives that we can really do what we want, right? Someday, even though we say we won't, we'll probably become these people who have to think about shit like jobs and house payments and all that crap, but right now . . . well, right now we can do anything. Think of all the things we can do. And . . ." He shakes his head like he's embarrassed. "I know it sounds stupid or whatever, but cutting my dreads made me feel like I'm ready for anything, you know what I mean? I'm ready to kind of leave all this." He gestures to everything around him.

"What, my bedroom is getting to be too much for you?" I ask. He laughs.

"No, you know what I mean. Just everything. This place. This town."

"Yeah, I know," I say, though I don't. Not really. I can't understand Joel's excitement for the future because I just want to escape the present. And I kind of envy and can't stand his enthusiasm.

I stare at his head and it makes me sad, too. I picture Lily cutting off his dreads, how they would just fall to the floor, cut off from Joel. And then get thrown out like they were never a part of him at all. I almost feel like asking him if he thought to put them in a box and bury them, like they rightfully deserved.

"Which is why your stupid ass should have found a place for us in Chicago while you were there," I say. "We could already be out of here."

He messes with his head again. "Right, I know. But like I said, I couldn't find a whole lot."

I pull at a stray piece of thread from my blanket.

"We'll figure it out," he says, and we sit there quietly. Suddenly he gets up and starts messing with the stuff on my corner night table.

"Hey," he says holding up an old picture, "this one's from my birthday?"

"Yeah," I say, though I don't really feel like reminiscing with Joel right now. I kind of wish he'd just leave.

The picture is one of him purchasing cigarettes. We made a big show of it and the guy at the counter thought we were freaks when I said to him, "Mama and Daddy and I are proud of this one," and I nodded in Joel's direction. "Our whole family's future is riding on him. Don't forget the lotto tickets, Brother!"

"Damn, French, that was so funny. How do you come up with shit like that?" Joel asks. We've laughed about that story countless times, so I know it's what he's referring to.

I shrug. "It's a gift," I say, even though it seems like a long time since I've been funny. I picture us that day, how we sat out-side scratching off lotto tickets, winning more free tickets, and then ten dollars that we used for a show that night.

"We saw the Purple Lemons that night," he says and puts down the picture. He picks up my book of Emily Dickinson's poems and leafs through it.

"Good band," I say.

"Yeah, good times, French."

"Yeah, good times."

"What's Em up to these days?" he says as he closes the book and sets it back down on my table.

"Oh, you know her. . . . Just some secret late-night cemetery raves," I answer.

"Cool," he says and smiles. The room gets quiet again and I wonder why this conversation with Joel suddenly feels so forced. Why he's been here ten minutes already and we're not listening to the Vinyls yet, or searching for cool new bands on the Inter-net. He sits down at the edge of my bed again.

"Oh, hey, I can't believe I forgot to tell you. So remember Lily's show at Zylos?"

Here we go again. I say, "Yeah."

"Well there was this agent there and he seemed pretty inter-ested in the band and got Sugar's info. Lily thought it was no big deal, but it turns out this guy is like a legit agent. And he's going to their show again tonight at the Stage."

The Stage. My stomach turns at the name of this other club downtown. "Uh, that's cool," I say. I pick up the remote and turn on the TV. My favorite animated movie that's been in the DVD player for the last few months flashes on the screen.

"*The Iron Giant*," Joel says, "I haven't seen this in forever."

"I'm sick of it," I lie as I switch to TV mode and start flipping through the channels.

"So, you'll be there, right? Lily can use all the support."

I stare at the screen. I hate that Joel assumes that I even want to support Lily. But even if I wanted to, there's no way I could go to that place ever again.

"Last time I went there, you totally ditched me," I remind him.

"What?" I stare at him. "Oh . . . yeah, that. Sorry," he says. I can't believe he almost forgot. That night we were all supposed to meet up and then he and Lily didn't show up. And I was there, alone. And that's why everything else went the way it did that night. "But that was forever ago. And I promise, I'll be there this time," he says.

Of course he will. That's where Lily will be.

"I'd go, but Robyn and I are seeing a movie tonight . . . ," I say. I figure I can convince Robyn to go to a movie instead.

"No, I talked to Robyn already," Joel looks at me with a confused expression. "She's going to the show so she can see Bobby."

"Oh . . . maybe she forgot," I say.

"Besides, I mean, this is like an agent." And the way he says it basically means that Lily's show is way more important than anything else. "It starts at ten but come earlier so we can hang out," he says, getting up. And even though I wished he would leave just moments ago, I also want him to stay. Now I want him to be here with me like he's always been, like I always thought he would be. If he could just stay in this room and not talk about Lily, not go on with his own life while I'm stuck in mine, and just be here so that I wouldn't be alone, that would help.

The phrase misery loves company runs through my head and I feel like a terrible human being.

"Hey," I say, "Want to go to Harold's?"

He smiles. "Aw, man. I wish I could. But I told Lily I'd be back to help her check the equipment and then we have to load it up and . . ." He stops himself.

"What, are you her roadie now or something?"

"Yeah, I know right?" he says, breezing through my sarcasm. But suddenly we're both quiet and there's an awkward silence again and he says, "But you know what, I can be late. It's no big deal. Just let me call Lily. . . ."

"No, no," I say, suddenly feeling like a pity case. "Go, it's no big deal."

"Are you sure?" he asks.

"Positive. Get out of here."

"Another time, okay? I promise."

"Yeah, sure," I say. "When we catch that movie together."

"Right," he says and smiles. "So, I'll see you later?"

"Later," I say. He leaves and I watch him go. And I don't know how he's done it, but Joel has managed to make me feel even more miserable than when he first walked in with his missing dreads. I can't even stand myself. I can't stand being in my own skin. I turn my attention back to the TV and flip through more channels. I wonder if Andy can see everything happening down here. What does he think of me now?

Chapter 10

I'm curious if Joel asked me to go to Lily's show because he really wants to hang out with me or if he's just worried about there being a good turnout. Or maybe he knows I don't have anything else better to do and feels sorry for me. I wish I had an excuse to get out of it, but I don't. I don't even have a job anymore. I got fired. Or maybe I quit. I'm still not really sure because I just walked out during my shift the day after Andy's funeral and never went back.

"Frenchie?" Mom says and comes into my room shortly after Joel leaves. I pull my covers over my head and pretend to be asleep because I don't feel like dealing with the question of why I'm still in bed.

"French?" she pulls the covers off and I look up to see her standing at the foot of my bed.

"What are you doing?" she asks, as if me lying in bed doesn't speak for itself. But she waits for an answer.

"I'm lying down, Mom," I say, wishing she'd go away.

She frowns. "Still?" I get irritated because it's such a stupid question. "Are you sick?" she asks.

"No, Mom. I just want to lie here is all."

"But in the middle of the day?" she says, like it's illegal.

"Do you need something?" I ask pulling the covers back over my head again and tucking them around me.

"No, you're just so quiet. I thought I'd make sure you weren't dead or something." She kind of laughs and I cringe because it's not funny. Some mothers do find their kids dead in their bedrooms.

"Why is it so dark in here? Open the window," she says, opening the blinds. "God, French. You can't just hole yourself up in here this way." Mom is not really the kind of person you can get rid of easily by mumbling nothing to. She will keep at it until you give her some kind of answer.

"I'm having a midlife crisis," I say from under the covers. The brightness of the light Mom has let in casts a reddish glow underneath my blanket. It's like I'm inside a hellish festive casket.

She laughs. "You're only seventeen. How can you be having a midlife crisis?"

"Maybe I'm going to die at thirty or something, in which case, I'm late."

"Don't say that." She's quiet for a minute, and I know she's staring at me. I can feel it. "Frenchie?" she says. I can picture her, standing there, with her hands on her hips. I make pretend snoring sounds. "Frenchie?" she presses again.

I know she's not going to leave unless I act semiserious.

I pull the blanket down. "Yes, Mother?" I say.

"Are you okay?" She looks at me with concern and it makes me feel both sad and guilty.

That cold, sweaty, nauseated feeling that makes you feel like you've eaten rotten oysters washes over me. I've never eaten oysters because they gross me out, but this is what I imagine it would feel like to eat bad ones. The acid from earlier creeps back up my throat.

"I'm fine," I say, because saying this means I don't have to really explain anything more.

She stands there silently for a moment before sitting on my bed. "You can't get depressed just because life kicks you down sometimes," she says softly. "You're an amazing girl." She looks around at my own paintings that I've hung up in my room. "Just look at these"—she says, shaking her head, and continues—"so you didn't get in. Big deal. You try again."

"Mom," I groan. "I'm still going to Chicago. I'm fine, really," I tell her. For somebody who doesn't want me to dwell on it, she sure does bring it up a lot.

"I know, I know. And I'm glad you'll get to take in the whole art scene there while you reapply. You have a plan, and it's a great plan, but I just hate to see the rejection . . . ," she says the word slowly, "get you down like this. I mean, you're at a point in your life where you really have everything ahead of you," she says. And the way she says this and smiles afterward, I know she actually believes it. I don't have the heart to tell her that I no longer imagine myself walking around Chicago, hanging out in cool coffeehouses and art galleries. All I see is me, in this bed, in this room, forever.

It's crazy how parents try to make you feel better and leave you feeling even more shitty than you did before.

"Thanks, Mom," I say. "And I promise, I'll get started on a new piece soon for the reapplication and everything. But right now, I'm just tired. Besides, I'm going to a show with Joel and Robyn later."

"Oh," she says and smiles, "a new piece is good. I can't wait to see it."

"I promise, Mom," I say.

"All right then. But I'm not going to let you stay in this room forever. Okay?"

"Okay," I say and Mom leaves. I roll over on my side and pull the blanket over my head again.

Chapter 11

I pull into one of the parking lots near the Stage and turn off the engine.

You can do this, I tell myself. I sit there wondering if I can really do this, if I can really go into this club again. But it's just a club. It's no big deal, right?

I take a deep breath, get out of the car, and start walking toward the Stage.

When I get to the line outside, the heavy feeling in my stomach somehow makes its way up to my chest. I close my eyes and take some deep breaths as I wait in line. The girl next to me is trying to look bored, but I can tell she's wondering what the hell is wrong with me.

I imagine gasping for breath and grabbing onto this girl's already torn fluorescent green shirt. She'd probably snarl at me and let me fall to the ground while her boyfriend watches with detachment and apathy. Then they'd probably just step over my sprawled out body on the sidewalk, as I make horrible sounds in my futile efforts to breathe.

I shake my head, trying to think normally again. I give the guy at the door my ID. He hands it back, slaps an "under 21" bracelet on my wrist, and waves me in. Except I don't move.

I'm paralyzed. I look inside and that night from four months ago comes rushing back to me. Everything is exactly the same as it was. The same reddish lights, the same mass of people. The same loud music.

"Are you going in or what?" the ID guy asks me impatiently.

The girl who was next to me is now behind me, and she's shoving her arm over me, waving her ID in the guy's face.

"Listen, if you're not going in . . . ," the guy says, ignoring her.

"I'm going, I'm going," I say and slowly walk in. Despite myself, despite my rational thinking, I look over to the far corner of the club, where I saw Andy that night. Part of me expects to see him there, staring back at me.

I can't believe I'm back here, and I briefly wonder if maybe I'm dreaming. I look around, taking everything in under the swirling red and gold lights. The Stage is two stories and has a red and gold theme. It reminds me of an old theater, which I guess is the reason for its name. The bottom floor has a huge audience area that is kind of lower than the stage. The stage is surrounded on either side by a few high tables with no chairs, and a bar directly across from it. The top story is balcony-like because it's recessed and you can see everything that's onstage and the audience below.

I look around for Joel, trying to spot him by his signature dreads, before remembering they're gone. Then I wonder if they really are, because being here somehow makes things surreal. I finally decide that if I'm dreaming, then Joel will still have his dreads. But if his hair is gone, then all of this must be an unfortunate reality. I spot Robyn, who is between Bobby and Colin, and head toward them reluctantly.

"Hey," I say.

"Yes! You're here," Robyn says and grabs me by the shoulders and jumps up and down. Bobby nods and Colin casually waves at me.

"OH MY GOD!" Robyn screams suddenly. I look in the direction she's looking and see Joel and Lily. They kiss before Lily heads onstage and Joel walks over to us.

"Where the hell are your dreads?" she says. Not dreaming.

"Gone," he says, rubbing his head with a grin on his face. "What do you think?" he asks her.

"You look like a white supremacist," she says and a hyena-type laugh escapes my lips. Joel is half-black and the idea of him looking like a white supremacist is totally absurd. I also get an evil pleasure hearing Robyn cut on Joel. Everyone looks at me and I clear my throat.

"Shut up, Robyn," Joel says, and shoves her a little.

"Relax, I'm just giving you a hard time," she says. "You look great! It seriously rocks and no offense, you were totally ready for it."

"That's what Lily said," he says. I want to punch Robyn for not hating it as much as I do.

"You guys don't know what you're talking about," I mumble.

"What's that, French?" Joel asks, leaning in.

"Nothing. I just think you looked perfectly fine with them," I say.

"Not that they weren't cool," Robyn insists. "They were just getting old. I think this is much better."

"Right," Joel says.

"I dunno," I say. "There's something to be said about staying true to oneself. Take old cars for instance. Look at my car. It's a good car. It's never let me down. And sure, a new one would be nice, but would it ever really be like my old car? I don't think so. Loyalty, kids. That's what it's all about."

They all stare at me once again with confused looks on their faces.

"What the fuck are you talking about?" Joel asks and then they all bust out laughing.

"Forget it," I say, and I can feel the heat of embarrassment and anger creeping into my cheeks.

Joel rolls his eyes at Robyn. I notice Colin looking at me and wearing an amused look.

Lily and her bandmates are onstage making adjustments to their instruments. She says something to them, jumps offstage, and comes over to us, making her typical round of hugs.

"French, you look adorable. Cool tights!" she says and points at the black spiderweb tights I'm wearing under some cutoff shorts.

Adorable. I suddenly feel like a kindergartener at a recital. But then I hear Andy's voice in my head, *Hey, cool tights*. I swallow hard as I suddenly realize I'd been wearing them that night. Did I do that on purpose?

"Are you okay?" Lily asks when I don't respond to her. Joel looks at me and his brow furrows. I need to act normal.

"Uh, yeah. And thanks!" I say with forced enthusiasm. "That means so much." But it comes out way more sarcastic and bitchy than intended.

Lily looks at me, and then over at Joel, who gets a funny look on his face, so I quickly say, "Just kidding!" and force a laugh.

"Is Bobby backstage?" Robyn cuts in. Lily nods. Robyn smirks and says, "Be right back, then!" and takes off for the stage.

"So I heard some agent is checking you guys out tonight," Colin says to Lily. "Is he here?"

She leans into Joel and he puts his arm around her. "Yep, sitting over there at the bar," she says and points in his direction and waves. We all turn to look at the same time and see a guy dressed in black lift a glass at us. He has shades on and looks like he's trying too hard to look cool and unimpressed. I feel like bursting Lily's bubble and telling her he's probably a fraud.

"I always thought short, bald, middle-aged men had all the power in the music industry," Colin says.

Lily laughs. "Oh, my! You better watch out, Joel."

They all laugh at her stupid joke.

"Well, we'll sit near him and keep him pumped while you're playing." Colin says to Lily.

"Aw thanks, Colin," she says and gives him a grateful look. "It's just, so much is riding on this. If he likes tonight's show, he might fly us out to California to record a demo. And if he really likes us, he'll tour us on the West Coast for a while to get us out there. He thinks we have a good West Coast appeal. Isn't that cool?"

Before I can stop my brain, an image of me socking Lily in the stomach flashes through my mind. I can't help it.

"That's pretty awesome," Colin says.

"Yeah, we're definitely excited," she answers and looks up at Joel. It takes me a few seconds to figure out what she means.

"What do you mean 'we'?" I say.

Colin looks back and forth between the two of us . . . actually, the three of us.

"French, I was going tell you," Joel starts. "But it kind of happened out of nowhere." He looks down and puts his hands in his pockets before saying, "I'm kind of going with Lily. Even if they don't get signed, Sugar is going to tour anyway, so . . ."

"So you're going with her," I finish for him.

He nods. "Yeah."

Lily glances back and forth between Joel and me and looks worried.

"I'm sorry, I didn't mean . . . ," she says.

"Don't worry about it," Joel says to her.

I don't say anything for a moment, as things start falling in place.

"So you never even looked for a place in Chicago this summer, right?" I say.

"I was going to, but . . . ," he says and looks back at Lily.

I nod. "I get it."

A guy who works here comes up to Lily. "We're ready for Sugar," he says.

She turns to me and says, "I'm really sorry, Frenchie. I thought you already knew," and she looks at Joel again.

"You can go ahead, Lil," Joel says. "I'll take care of this."

My blood boils. I am *this*?

"Okay, well, wish me luck," she whispers to Joel, and he gives her a kiss.

"You'll be great," he tells her. And then she jumps up onstage and starts talking to the band.

"Of course you will," I mutter.

"Frenchie . . . ," Joel starts.

"Joel," I say, "Just drop it." He sucks in his breath and shakes his head, but says nothing more.

Robyn suddenly appears and jumps offstage, crashing into me. "They're gonna start," she yells. I look over at Joel.

"Come on," Colin says and motions me to get closer to the stage. Robyn and Joel walk beside us.

"Hi, everyone, we're Sugar." Lily's throaty voice booms throughout the Stage. Out of the corner of my eye I see Joel watching her. He's forgotten about me, and it's all about Lily again.

I wonder if I can bad juju their performance. I want the crowd to boo her and demand that she and her ridiculously named band get off the stage. But even if all those things happen, Joel still won't be moving to Chicago and my only plan is completely ruined. Even though it already was.

Bobby bangs his drumsticks together and yells, "Two, three, four!"

And the place explodes. The song they open with is different

than the other night, but it's just as addictive. People start dancing, many of them singing along with Lily. Everyone is moving
and Lily dances like she doesn't care about anything.

And damn it if it's not one of their best performances. Agent
Guy is nodding his head to the music as he watches Sugar and the
crowd. I see a slight smile on his face and know he loves them.
Despite all my bad juju, he loves them.

In a break between songs, Joel yells, "I LOVE YOU, LILY!"

She winks at him and blows him a kiss before going into the
next song, and the next, and the next. And with each one, I get
more and more pissed.

Finally, their set is over and Lily exits the stage.

"Babe, you guys kicked ass! This guy would be crazy not to
sign you!" Joel says when she heads back over to us several minutes later. He's grinning and looks so damn excited.

"I thought we were good," Lily says, "but I mean, it's hard to
tell when you're up there—"

"You were great, Lily," I cut in and move in closer to her.

"Thanks, Frenchie," she says. "And I really am sorry—"

"You were fantastic," I say, cutting her off again. "Absolutely
amazing. In fact, Lily, I don't think there's anyone who could ever
top you. . . ."

"Frenchie," Joel says.

Lily doesn't say anything and just looks at the ground.

"Stop," Joel says, staring me down and I hold his gaze for a minute.

"Whatever. I'm getting out of here," I say and start shoving my way past him.

I feel like a scab. Like a big loser scab.

Joel grabs my arm. "French, stop. We gotta talk."

"No," I say, pulling my arm back. "Clearly you've gotten everything all figured out."

Joel looks at me. "What the hell is your problem? I'm trying to talk to you."

"Just forget it," I say.

"No, I don't want to forget it. I know you're pissed and I get it. I should have told you sooner. It's just hard when you never want to hang out, so how was I—"

"Wait? What? Just hold on one fucking second, Joel," I say. "You're the one who bailed. You're the one who's too wrapped up in his own life to care about anything else."

"What the hell is that supposed to mean?" he says. I stare at Lily. "So what, French? Am I supposed to apologize because I'm happy? That's really shitty, you know that? And I am sorry. I'm sorry you're bitter and miserable and you can't be happy for me."

"Right! Oh, okay, yeah, Joel. That's it. It couldn't possibly be that whenever you 'fall in love' you forget about everything and

everyone else in your life until you end up scaring the girl away,"
I say, firing off the quote mark gestures like guns. "Let's see,
before you brought Punk Rock Barbie here," I say pointing at
Lily, "there was Julie, and then Kenso, and then that hippie chick.
Or were those different?"

Joel is glaring at me but I can't stop. "Weren't you in love all
those times, too?" I say.

"This is different," he says through clenched teeth. Lily
comes over and looks at me, her mouth wide open and her face
frozen in shock by the words coming out of my mouth.

"Joel . . . ," she says. Joel shakes his head and looks like I am
the devil's spawn.

"You know what, Frenchie? You're a real fucking bitch," he
says. He says it like he's never been more certain of anything.

"Yeah? Well, you're an asshole," I spit back, "especially since
she came into the picture."

"Just shut the hell up," Joel says.

"If it weren't for her, you would've been here that night the
way you said you would be!"

"Lily, let's go," he says, and turns to leave.

"That's not fair. YOU didn't show up! And now you're bail-
ing on me again," I yell.

"Whatever Frenchie. We're done," he says, like it's final.

Joel leaves and he doesn't look back once.

"FUCK YOU, JOEL!" I yell after him. I'm so pissed and I have so much adrenaline pulsing through my body right now that I'm shaking. Robyn pulls my arm and starts leading me out of the club and Colin follows us out.

Once we're outside, Robyn keeps telling me to relax but I'm fuming. "Robyn, that's so unfair!" I yell at her and I'm on the verge of crying, but I won't.

"What the hell was that?" Colin says.

"That," I say, "was a dose of the truth!"

Robyn looks at me the way people do when they know you're wrong but don't want to tell you.

"Come on, Robyn, please," I say. "I mean, aren't I right?"

"I guess," she says. "But French, that was pretty harsh. Even for you." She shakes her head.

"Are you kidding? You don't even get it." My rage bubbles up again.

"Okay, okay, okay," Robyn says. "Just relax."

Colin and Robyn look at each other.

"Let's just go," Robyn advises.

When we get to my car, Robyn asks, "Do you want me to drive you home?"

"No," I answer.

"It's no big deal."

"No, it's fine," I tell her as I get my keys out. It's totally ridiculous that she thinks I'm too upset to drive.

"Come on, just let me." She tries to grab the keys from my hand.

"Stop," I say. "Seriously, I'm fine." I try to seem fine.

Robyn looks doubtful and persists. "I just think . . ."

"Damn it, Robyn! I said I'm fine," I snap at her before she has a chance to finish. She gives me a look, and I know I've pissed her off now, too.

Colin stands there looking uncertain about what he should do.

"Fine. You're fine," she says. "I'm going back, then." She turns and heads back in the direction of the club without saying anything else, leaving Colin and me alone.

I sigh. "Robyn!" I call, but she's already halfway down the block. Another friend bites the dust.

"I better go," I say to Colin and open my car door, signaling the go-ahead for him to leave also.

"Uh . . . yeah, okay." He looks like he wants to say something else but isn't sure if he should. "Listen . . . do you maybe want to go somewhere?" he says.

I shake my head and laugh because I can't imagine anyone wanting to go anywhere with me right now. "Yeah, as you can see, I'm wonderful company."

He shrugs. "I mean, you just look like you could use a friend or something right now." He looks genuinely concerned, which makes my face flush with embarrassment.

"Thanks," I say and shake my head. "But I should probably just go home."

He takes out his phone and fiddles with it for a minute. "Okay, but if you change your mind," he says and suddenly my phone in my pocket starts ringing. "That's me," he says and hangs up. "Now you have my number. So, if you want to talk or something, you can give me a call."

"Okay, thanks," I say and nod. "Wait. How do you have my number?"

He shifts his gaze and says, "Uh, Robyn gave it to me that night at Zylos."

"Oh," I say wondering why Colin hadn't erased it yet after witnessing my numerous displays of being a total jerk. "Well, thanks," I say.

"Yeah, sure," he says.

I get in my car and start it up. Colin steps aside as I pull away.

As I drive, my mind gets crowded with everything that just happened. I can't stop thinking about the things Joel said, and the things I said. I'm suddenly aware of how I was yelling. How out of control I must have looked. How Robyn had to take me outside. And then, how I yelled at her. My eyes start to fill up with tears, but I wipe at them quickly.

I open the windows. The hot night air rushes in and with it, Andy's words from that night.

I like this, driving at night with the windows open, he had yelled over the sound of the wind.

Me, too, I yelled back, secretly adding another mark to the invisible tally I'd been keeping of all the ways Andy and I were alike and what it might mean. It was dark and my hair was whipping into my eyes, but I looked over at him and he was looking at me. There was something in that look that filled me with some kind of mixed happiness and sadness. There was *something* in that look, but the wind was too loud for talking. He had already leaned his head back and closed his eyes and there was nothing more to say.

I looked back at the road and the wind whistled louder. The music filled the car and I headed deeper into the night with Andy Cooper by my side, foolishly thinking we were driving into some kind of destiny.

I turn up the music now, as loud as it will go, until the pounding in my head matches the beat of the song. It aches so much. I don't want to be able to remember anymore.

But I do.

I remember everything. I remember Andy.

Chapter 12

When I get home, I turn down the music and sit in the driveway. Against my better judgment, I text Joel.

Hey, tonight sucked. We should talk.

I wait, but nothing.

I know you're pissed.

Still no reply.

So I guess ur just never gonna talk
to me again?

Nothing.

Fine. Have a nice life.

And with that, I'm pretty sure my friendship with Joel is over. I look toward the cemetery. Sadly, I think Em is now my best friend.

I take out my wallet and slip out a newspaper clipping. It's Andy Cooper's obituary, already worn from all the times I've read it since the day I carefully tore it out of Harold's morning paper. It was like any other morning, except it wasn't. I scan it in its entirety and then reread the first couple of sentences several times, like I always do.

```
Andrew James Cooper, 18, of Orlando, passed
away in his sleep at his home. He is survived
by   his   mother,   father,   brother,   and
grandparents. Andrew was a lover of words and
ideas, and he was a seeker of truth.
```

Passed away in his sleep. It almost sounds nice. It almost sounds like he was carried away on a dream and woke up in a better place and decided not to come back. It almost sounds like he could wake up if he wanted to. But then I guess putting something like *Andy killed himself and all we got was a lousy suicide note* would probably be inappropriate even if it was true.

Nobody knows I cut this out and keep it in my wallet. I don't know why I do because I kind of hate Andy's obituary. I think it's the "seeker of truth" that I hate most. It makes him sound so noble and better than us, like he died in the name of searching for truth.

The valedictorian must have read it too, because she used those exact words in her graduation speech. It jolted me when she said them, and I got pissed as she presented those words to mean something more than they really did. She advised us to be seekers of our own truths, to search within ourselves and find out what we were passionate about, and then go out there and share that passion in some way with the world. And if we did this, the world would be a better place. She spoke like we all had certain futures. She spoke like none of us would fail, none of us would get lost, none of us would give up.

Everyone applauded. They looked at her like she was a hero who'd offered us all some kind of salvation. They feasted on those words meant for a dead boy with no future. It suddenly seemed like Andy and what he had done couldn't touch us. We were not him. None of us could be him. Look at us, we were here. Our futures were guaranteed. Everyone's parents breathed a sigh of relief.

I sat there in a stupor, surrounded by all these people, and wondered, where was the despair? Why didn't they tell us what to do when life becomes so crippling that all you can do is kill yourself? What were you supposed to do when you felt that way? I stared at the row where Andy would have been. All the seats were filled. No empty chair to remind us. No despair. No words about this. Just a diploma and a kick in the ass before we all realized how ill-equipped we really were.

And besides, what the hell was this truth? I suffered through a speech that guaranteed we'd find it in ourselves, and yet, Andy never did. Or did he think he had to die to find it? Did that mean life was just a huge lie to him?

If Andy really thought that, then that night, the night he said would be some great adventure, the last night he was alive . . . he was just fucking with me.

Chapter 13

I go inside my house and straight to my bedroom. I turn on the TV and crawl under my red blanket. The familiar dialogue of *The Iron Giant* fills the room. Without the pounding music filling up my head, Joel's words come back and make me feel terrible all over again.

I think about how messed up things have gotten. Each day I just want to be isolated in this room more and more. That would be so much easier. Maybe I can lock myself in here and my parents can bring a tray of food to my door. Every day I can just sit here, peering out my window and painting pictures. And then all the kids can be scared of me and make up scary stories about me.

But my parents won't be around forever, which means I'll be alone, in this house, for decades. Maybe nobody will even know when I die in here, like the old man across the street. Maybe I'll just rot in this room.

My phone buzzes with an incoming text. I quickly reach for it hoping it's Joel.

It's not.

> Hey, it's Colin. Just making sure you got
> home okay.

I cringe because he apparently thinks I'm a raging dumbass. It really sucks for someone to witness you at your worst.

Then another text comes in.

> Uh, I don't mean you're a crazy person. Ur
> not. Not really.

I sigh. I'm just about to text back when another text comes in.

> And now you probably think I'm a weirdo bc
> I've sent you two texts in less than a
> minute.

Actually...

> Actually 3. And this makes 4. And now you
> think I'm crazy. But I just wanted to make
> sure you got home okay.

I start texting back, but then another text comes in.

> I'm not.

I'm wondering what that means when I get the rest of the text.

> Crazy. Or a stalker. This is bad. Can you
> delete all of these, please? I'm stopping
> now.

Despite feeling horrible, I smile as another one buzzes in.

Basically, I just hope you're okay.

I'm fine, I text back. And send more texts indi-
vidually.

I didn't run over anyone.

Thanks for checking.

I don't think you're crazy or a stalker.

I guess you're all right.

Thanks for hanging around.

I'm not a stalker either.

I wait to see if he responds. He does.

No problem.

I text back.

Goodnight, Colin.

Goodnight, Frenchie.

I lie back down and stare at my ceiling, replaying tonight over and over again. I see me and Joel at the Stage, yelling at each other. And Lily standing there with that stupid look on her face.

I close my eyes to shut out those images, but when I do, I see flashes of Andy Cooper. I see snapshots of that night and how I must have missed something. If I could just go back and find out what I missed . . . it would somehow give me the power to change it. I would wake up in a new day, where none of this had happened. Where I somehow saved him. And my life, everything, would make sense again.

If what happened with Andy Cooper had never happened then everything would be different. I would be different and then maybe this night with Joel wouldn't have gone down the way it did.

But I also can't help thinking, if Joel had never met Lily, if he'd been there the night I ran into Andy, then that night would never have happened the way it did either.

I don't even know what to think anymore and I just want to fall asleep and think of nothing.

I close my eyes again, but this time I see the blonde woman peering down at me in the middle of the dance floor. *Is that Frenchie? Is that girl's name Frenchie?*

I open my eyes. It's useless. I roll out of bed, let myself flop onto the floor, and stay there.

I'm crazy. Had he said that or was I just imagining it? Was Andy crazy? Would he have killed himself no matter what? Or could I have changed it somehow?

What did I miss?

I look at my clock. Midnight. The red numbers click to 12:01 and the swirl of the red and gold lights at the Stage plays back in my head. And the way I felt when I walked in there again.

I hold in my breath.

My heart races as my mind comes up with a crazy plan. I

wonder if I should, if I can do it.

I watch the minutes pass as I try to work up the courage. But it doesn't matter, because it's not courage that makes me reach for the phone. It's those minutes ticking by and the knowing that I can't stay here, waiting for another morning, where I'll wake up and try to find reasons to get out of bed.

I hold my phone and start tapping away before I can change my mind.

R u there?

I wait, hoping he'll text back. A moment later, my phone buzzes with an incoming text.

I'm here. What's up?

I'm not okay.

When I see those words typed out, I realize the truth of them. I let them register for a minute knowing more than ever that I have to go through with this. I keep typing.

I need to figure out something. And I need a favor. It's kind of crazy.

OK . . . ?

Will u meet me at the corner of my block? Same block as Greenwood Cemetery. Do u know where that is?

Now?

Yes.

Sure. What should I do when I get there?

Just wait. Then I'll tell you the rest.

OK . . . b there in 15.

Chapter 14

Fifteen minutes later, I've checked to make sure my parents aren't awake. I turn off my light and slowly open my window, every muscle in my body tensing at the slightest squeak.

Once outside, I walk around the side of my house and run down to the corner. I already see a car waiting there and I pray that it's Colin's. I peer inside as I get closer and see that he's looking for me. He smiles when he sees me and I open the door.

"Hey," I say as I get in, suddenly embarrassed about asking Colin to meet me here. The longest conversation we've ever had was fifteen minutes ago via text messages.

"Hey," he says. I can tell he's a little nervous too. "So, I'm here. First part is done, now will you tell me what you need?"

I don't know how to say it without it sounding incredibly creepy. It seems impossible to try and explain everything all at once. I take a deep breath and hope my explanation is enough.

"I know this is going to sound crazy. But maybe you already

think I am crazy, so it won't even matter at this point. . . . I just, I have to do this thing," I tell him. I can hear the way my voice goes up at the end of my sentence. I'm irritated with how nervous I sound.

"Hey," he says, "it's okay. Whatever you need to do, we'll do it. Okay?"

"Okay," I say and I turn to look at him. "I just need you to hang out with me tonight, to have one night of adventure. See, I barely know you and that's what makes it so perfect. Because I need to figure something out, and I think this is the only way to do it," I tell him. "I basically just have to finish tonight. And there's no backing out."

He looks at me oddly. I know he wants to ask me what the hell that even means, but instead he says slowly, "Okay."

I nod, relieved. "Okay then."

"So where to?"

"The Stage."

He raises an eyebrow, but says, "The Stage it is." He shifts the car into drive.

Chapter 15

We pull into the nearest parking lot. Colin turns off the engine and starts to get out of the car, but I don't. I'm suddenly terrified of facing that place again.

Colin looks over at me. "You ready?"

I shake my head. He waits, but after awhile, he gets out. I watch as he comes over to my side and opens the door.

"Come on," he says.

"Hold on," I say. He stands there while I sit and try to think. "It's just . . . nothing about tonight is going to make sense," I say. "And it's more than kind of crazy. It's sort of . . . demented." I suddenly realize how warped this is, how I'm basically trying to chase down a ghost. "Maybe it's not fair of me to ask you to be part of it."

He stares at me. "You're a really strange girl, Frenchie."

"I know," I say. "And I'm probably only going to seem stranger after tonight."

"Well," he says and looks out at the parking lot. I sit and wait, sure he will get back in the car and drive my strange, demented ass home. But instead he leans down and looks directly at me. "A few things: I don't mind strange. And I'm already a part of this. No backing out, right?"

I stare back at him and know that Colin will probably take me anywhere I ask him tonight. But not back home. Not yet.

"So," he says. "Let's go."

I take a deep breath, will myself to move, and finally get out of the car.

We head toward the Stage and I get the same feeling I did earlier. That sense of déjà vu. I'm walking to the Stage now, with Colin, but somewhere else, I'm walking to the Stage alone and my whole night with Andy is just about to begin.

I turn and look over my shoulder, half expecting to see Andy, but only Colin is there, looking at me.

When we get to the door, we flash our wristbands from earlier and the guy at the door lets us in.

"You ready?" Colin asks. I nod and we go inside.

Sugar's equipment is no longer onstage, and the music is now being provided by a DJ set up in the far corner of the room. The music he's spinning is loud and pulsing and the place is dark without the bright lights from the stage. The few lights that are flashing are just like in my dream, just like that night, and I feel like I've found a wormhole somehow. Like I might actually be able to step back and forth, between now and then. I have a strange desire to go to the middle of the dance floor and lie down, just to see if it will open up and swallow me. Maybe Andy will be in that hole. Maybe I can finally ask him what I've been dying to know.

Lily and Joel are dancing and Robyn and Bobby are making out. I slowly make my way around the outside of the crowd, hoping they don't notice me. Colin follows. I stop in front of the wall at the far end of the club, opposite the stage, where you go if you don't want the lights of the dance floor to hit you. Where you go if you don't want to be seen. I lean closer to Colin and say, "Will you wait here for me? I'll be right back."

He nods. "Yeah, sure. I'll be right here," he says.

"And don't let any of them see you," I say and gesture toward Joel, Lily, and Robyn. "I don't want them to know I'm back."

He looks out at the group. "Okay."

I turn around and set my eyes on the red velvet curtain that covers a doorway on the wall to my right. I make my way toward it, not knowing exactly what is on the other side, but knowing this is where I need to start. And somehow, behind that curtain, is the opening to the wormhole that will lead me to that other night. The night where Andy is still alive, the night where nothing has happened yet.

PART 2

WILD NIGHTS— WILD NIGHTS!

Chapter 16

Have you ever been sitting outside and the mailman shows up with a package for you? It's awesome because you weren't expecting it, and you feel special. You feel awesome. You feel excited as the mailman delivers it, all pretty with a bow. And he sets it down right in front of you with a smile and a tip of his hat.

You pull the bow, but here's what's inside:

One of those little black bombs with a burning fuse at the end, like the kind you see in cartoons. You're stunned. You run up to the mailman and say, "Dude, I don't want this!" You try to give it back, but he just pushes it back to you, and so on and so forth, and during all that time the fuse is getting shorter and shorter. Finally he just drives away, and you're standing there, holding this little bomb in your hand, just waiting for the boom.

That was me.

Andy Cooper was the boom.

Chapter 17

THAT NIGHT

I arrive at the Stage about ten minutes before the Tantrums are scheduled to go on. The place is already packed. People are standing around, waiting and talking to each other. I look around for Joel, because he and Lily are supposed to meet me here.

I don't see them anywhere, and actually, I don't get why Joel couldn't hang without Lily. They'd only met last week, but already they were together 24/7. But whatever, at least he is going to come. I hate being at shows by myself.

I walk around trying to draw as little attention to myself as possible in the attempt to not look like some loser who doesn't have friends. Still no Joel and Lily, so I find an empty space near the door. I take out a cigarette and light up so I'll at least have something to do with my hands. I keep watch of the door, waiting for Joel and Lily to show up.

Twenty minutes later, the Tantrums still haven't taken the

stage and there's no sign of Joel or Lily. I'm pissed and on my third cigarette.

I throw the cigarette butt on the floor and put it out with my shoe, then scrounge around in my bag for gum, but only find a slightly opened apple Jolly Rancher. I wipe the lint and crumbs off of it, unwrap it, and pop it in my mouth.

I look toward the door again for the hundredth time. And that's when I see him.

Not Joel, but Andy Cooper.

I watch him walk across the room, in his wrinkled button-down shirt and khaki shorts. People stop to stare at his ridiculous outfit. He meets their gazes as he walks by them. I keep my eyes on him, tracking him by his brownish blond hair, and then he disappears behind the red velvet curtain on the far side of the room.

I take a deep breath and tell myself to relax. It's stupid to get this worked up over a guy.

The Tantrums finally take the stage. The lead singer has flaming orange hair that is impressively spiked and sticking up a good six inches from his scalp. He's skinny and pale, which means he probably shouldn't wear that leather jacket without a shirt underneath, but somehow it works. He doesn't work the crowd at all. The band just immediately starts playing and he starts yelling into the microphone like he's possessed. He jumps and throws himself all over the stage and the crowd loves it. I can see he's bleeding, but he just bangs his head around some more and screams.

I groan. This is bad, but most of the crowd seems to be enjoying their stupid antics. I crane my neck and look for Joel again. I'm pretty sure that he's not coming at this point and I probably just got ditched for whatever better thing he's doing with Lily.

Somehow I've ended up in the middle of the floor, having been pushed closer to the stage with everyone trying to get closer. I finally make it back to the edge of the throng of idiots and press up against the safety of the wall while people continue jumping and thrashing around. I look over to the red velvet curtain and notice Andy Cooper coming back through it.

Some sketchy guy wearing glasses follows behind him. They talk for a minute before the sketchy guy goes to the bar. Andy reaches for something in his pocket, a flask, and takes a swig from it.

I never would have pegged Andy Cooper for having a flask and boozing it up on the weekends. He takes another swig, puts it away, and then looks around the room and notices me. He smiles and just kind of stares at me for a moment.

The obvious thing to do when the guy you've had a crush on for the past four years looks at you and smiles is to smile back. Or maybe even wave. Someone like Robyn could pull off a wink. But me, I look away and pretend I didn't see him. I think I might have actually accidentally scowled.

I look at the stage for a minute, then I look back to where Andy was standing, but he's gone. My stomach drops and I curse myself for being such a moron.

"Frenchie," I hear on the other side of me. I look over and there's Andy, tall and beautiful and incredibly close.

"Andy. Andy Cooper. How the hell are you?" I say this with too much gusto and like a fucking forty-year-old salesman running into an old college buddy. I'm surprised I didn't give him a slap on the back and a handshake. He smiles and shrugs. "I thought it was you, but I wasn't sure."

"It's me," I say, as if it weren't obvious.

"Yeah . . . ," he says. "That's what I thought. So, are you a fan?" He gestures to the Tantrums onstage.

"Me? No, just thought I'd check them out. I was supposed to meet a friend here."

"Oh, sorry . . . ," he says. My ears burn and I know I'm turning all shades of red. I'm glad it's dark in here.

"No, I mean, not like a guy or anything. Well, yes, a guy. But not like a guy . . . guy. It's not like I got stood up or anything. I mean, not in the conventional girl/guy kind of way. It's not that," I say. "I'm supposed to meet Joel. You know Joel Borneut, right?"

I'm jittery and saying too much, but Andy just nods and watches the band onstage while I bite at a hangnail.

"Yeah, yeah, I know him," he says. "Good guy."

"Yeah, good guy who just ditched me to hang out with his new girlfriend," I blurt out.

"That sucks," he says. "People disappoint, Frenchie." He takes the flask out again and offers it to me.

I shake my head. "No thanks." He shrugs and takes another swig.

"I thought this stuff might numb the terribleness of this band, but they're still pretty bad," he says.

I look over at the stage and notice the Tantrums' lead singer is on his back, writhing like he's in pain and making his way from one side of the stage to the other.

"Yeah," I say. "I'll probably ditch soon." And realize too late that hanging out with Andy has been the best part of my evening, and I should be trying to make this moment last.

"Yeah, me too," Andy says, but neither of us leave. I should leave. I should rescue him from my awkward company. But instead, I just stand next to him and listen to the terrible Tantrums some more.

"Do you come here often?" I ask him because I feel I should say something.

"Sometimes," he says.

"Cool," I answer.

Despite their total lack of talent, I focus all of my attention back on the band, just so I can stop focusing on how close Andy Cooper is standing next to me.

But after a few minutes, I sneak a look over at him. His eyes are closed and he's leaning his head back against the wall. I notice the line of his jaw, straight and strong. If I moved closer to him and tilted my head back, too, my lips would reach his chin perfectly. Suddenly, he opens his eyes and catches me looking at him.

And of course I look away.

I open my mouth to say something, anything to shift the attention from my awkwardness.

"This band really sucks . . . ," I say even though we've already established this. But he's saying something too, and even though the music is screeching and I was talking over him, I know I hear it.

". . . hang out for a while?"

"What?" I say, leaning in closer so that I can hear him clearly. So I don't make a fool of myself by thinking he said what I think he said.

He leans in closer, so close that I can feel his breath on my ear and smell the alcohol. He says it again, "Do you want to hang out?"

"Uh . . . sure," I say. "But aren't we kind of already doing that?" Nice, Frenchie.

He laughs. "Right. But I meant, like, let's go. Let's get out of here. Let's . . ." He pauses and smiles. "Have one cool night."

"One cool night . . . ," I repeat.

"One night of whatever, you know? One night of something more than this." He gestures around at the place and the people around us. "One night to do anything and go anywhere. . . ." His blue-green eyes look glassy, and I know it's probably the alcohol, but maybe they're also bright with anticipation.

I don't say anything immediately. I stare at the band disinterestedly and say, "Well . . . ," like I'm considering it.

"Come on," he says.

I look at him and smile. And then he smiles back. Suddenly it feels like Andy Cooper and I are in on this great big secret together.

"Let's go," I say finally.

He grins. "Let's go."

Chapter 18

TONIGHT

I go through the red velvet curtain and notice it's much darker in here than the main area. It looks like it's just a long hallway. I blink a few times, letting my eyes adjust, and run my hand down the cold brick. I know this is where I saw Andy come out that night with the guy who I'm pretty sure went to our school years ago. I continue walking down the hall, but don't see anyone and wonder if this is a stupid idea. I feel the bass and drums thumping through my hand as I feel my way down the hall. I feel another curtain to my right and peek through it. Another hallway. Somewhere I hear voices, but they sound like they're coming through the walls. I bite my lip and wonder if I should keep going further into the darkness, or through this curtain and down this other hall. I opt for the new direction.

"What are you doing back here?" I spin around and some big muscle-head guy is towering over me.

The guy is intimidating, but I try to act like I belong here.

"I'm looking for someone," I say.

He looks at me expectantly with his arms on his hips, which looks kind of funny because he's huge—like a chastising mama gorilla.

"Who?" he asks.

"A really skinny guy, with dark-rimmed glasses. And he's scruffy."

"Sid? You're looking for Sid?"

I have no idea if I'm looking for Sid or not, but I nod. "Yeah, Sid. I gotta talk to him."

He stares me down. "You know Sid?"

I scowl. "Yes, and he told me he'd be here." I cross my arms. "Is he here or not?"

The guy eyes me a little longer and then says, "Down that hall, out the back exit . . . like always."

"Right, thanks," I say as he moves past me. I backtrack and find my way to the original hall I was in.

I think of Andy and wonder if he ran into Mama Gorilla. Did he get asked the same questions? Or did he fist bump Mama Gorilla as he passed him in the hall?

I head toward the red exit sign down the hall. Somebody comes in through the door and makes his way toward me. It's too dark to see if it's Sid, so as he passes, I whisper, "Sid?" figuring he'll stop if it's him.

"Back there," the dark figure answers. I push open the door at the end of the hall. It leads to a dark back alley, barely illuminated with a backlight near the door.

I don't see anybody as I step outside, and I'm only the slightest bit aware of how stupid it is to go into dark alleys alone looking for some sketchy guy.

I look around, but see no one.

"Sid?" I try.

Nothing. And my whole plan starts to undo before it even begins.

"Sid?" I say again.

"Who the fuck wants to know?" comes a voice from the far right side of the alley.

"Uh, I do."

"And who the hell is 'I'?" says the voice again.

I pause and wonder if I should turn around and go back inside before this gets all screwed up. Finally, somebody emerges from the other side of a Dumpster I hadn't noticed. He's rail thin and sketchy-looking. It's Sid. "Frenchie," I say.

"What do you want?" he says, crossing his arms over his chest.

Now that he's in front of me, and there's not some voice coming from the darkness, I realize what a tiny guy he is. Even though he's taller than me, he's probably half my weight and he looks frail. I could probably break him in half. "You know Andy Cooper?" I ask.

"What's it to you?" He answers all streetwise.

"He's a friend. He told me I'd find you here," I say.

"Oh yeah? And how exactly did he tell you? Did he reach out to you from the great beyond?" He says and stares at me. I'm taken off guard for a minute because he knows. I resume my composure and go on.

"Listen, I know he came to you about four months ago. I was with him. Now all I want is some of the same stuff, okay?"

He looks at me for a while and then says, "You better not be setting me up," and he looks over his shoulder.

"I'm not," I say, "just help me out, okay?"

"Fuck you," he says. He turns his back on me and starts walking away.

"NO!" I yell, and start following him, "Listen to me," I say. He turns around. "I know you sold to him that night and all I'm asking is for you to do the same, okay? Just sell me what you sold him. I don't give a shit, I just want the same."

He stares at me for a second before saying, "You want to end up like Andy?"

I shrug, "Maybe."

"He went on a wild ride," he says. I shrug again. "Let me see the cash."

I pull out my wallet and show him what I have. He reaches over and grabs all of it before looking around again and going into his pocket. He pulls out a small bag filled with all kinds of pills and tosses it to me.

"Chase it with some liquor, they'll work better."

"Thanks," I say, putting them in my now empty wallet.

"Andy was a good guy," he says suddenly. "Pretty fearless. If you see him"—he says with a grin—"tell him Sid said hi. Now get lost." And with that he turns around and heads back toward the Dumpster and leaves me standing there. "Go!" he yells back. I turn around and head back inside.

I go down the hall again, toward the loud thumping music, somehow feeling different with the pills in my wallet.

I go through the red curtains again and into the crowded room of dancing people. I feel like I know something they don't.

I spot Colin.

"Let's go," I say as I walk past him and back outside.

Chapter 19

THAT NIGHT

Andy and I leave the Stage together and head to my car, but we pass a little shop on Orange Avenue with a flashing sign advertising tarot and palm readings. Andy stops in front of it and says, "What do you say, Frenchie, adventurous one? Do you want to know your future?"

"I don't know. It's always seemed like such a scam to me," I say. "I mean, don't you think whatever they say, you have the power to change? You could leave there and do the opposite of what they say, so then what's the point?"

"I don't know. I figure some things are gonna happen no matter what," he says. "Come on, let's check it out."

"I dunno. Aren't you scared you'll go in there and she'll tell you something horrible? Like you're going to get in an accident or die?" I say.

"I guess I'm the kind of person who would want to know," he says.

"Fine," I say. Andy reaches for my hand and I catch my breath as his fingers lace with mine. He opens the door and the sound of wind chimes fills the air.

As soon as we walk in, I smell an overwhelming variety of incense. There's a ton of wind chimes hanging all over and rows and rows of weird knickknacks, incense burners, crosses, and books. We're the only ones in the tiny store.

A woman with long black hair peppered with gray comes out from behind a curtain.

"Good evening," she says. "Can I help you two?"

I look over at Andy. This is his idea, his adventure.

"Uh, is this where we can get a reading?"

"Yes, yes, of course. It's ten dollars for a palm reading, fifteen for tarot, and twenty for psychic," says the woman.

I look at Andy. "Forget it," I tell him. Like I need to pay twenty dollars to be told I'm going to die.

"We'll take a psychic reading. Each," he says and pulls a hundred dollar bill from his pocket. "My treat," he says to me as the woman goes to the register.

"What the hell?" I say. "Do you always carry that much money with you?"

"Not always."

The woman returns with Andy's change, and then goes to the door and flips the sign from OPEN to CLOSED.

"Who's first?" she asks.

"You," Andy says to me.

"Me? Why not you?"

"Just go," he says, and since the old woman is standing there waiting on one of us, I shake my head and say, "Fine."

The woman smiles and tells me to follow her. She leads me through the curtains, and to a little room with a table and two chairs. She tells me to sit down, and then she sits across from me.

"Try to relax," she says. "I will tell you what I see. I will tell you good and bad." I get nervous when she says this. What if she gives me an age? An actual age? The psychic asks me for my hand, which I offer slowly. She puts her hands over my open palms, closes her eyes, and takes some deep breaths. I look at her wrinkled hands, almost translucent and covered with brown age spots. I look at her face, deep in concentration, and wonder if I should also close my eyes. But I want to catch any change in her expression, so when she feels sorry for me and lies by telling me I have a bright future, I'll know it's not true. She opens her eyes and looks at me.

"I sense you are an old soul," she says. "You have been on this earth before. You have had many lives. You are a wise, creative individual." She closes her eyes again. "But you will lose your focus. Something will happen and the uncertainty you already feel will multiply tenfold."

She opens her eyes again and looks straight at me, "I worry for you."

Now I know the one thing you don't want a psychic to say to you is, "I worry for you." My stomach drops. What the hell is she seeing?

She continues with, "I sense darkness around you. I sense . . . emptiness."

Does this woman have anything good to tell me?

"You are looking for direction in your life right now. You have blurry plans. And something or someone unexpected will have a great impact on them," she says, looking straight at me. "It will throw you and your plans into much confusion."

She sighs. "I sense you will have much to overcome in the near future. You will begin to question many things," she says. "But you are capable of making wise decisions. And you are quite sensitive, which means you feel deeply, more than most, and sometimes your feelings can overwhelm you." She looks at me as if that should settle it. "Do you have any questions?"

Do I have any questions? Uh, yeah. What the hell kind of reading was that?

But instead I say no because I'm trying to remember every-thing she said, but I can already feel it slipping away since it mostly sounded like a riddle.

"Okay," she says and waits. I assume this is my cue to get up, but then she says, "Close your eyes."

I do.

"Think on something, something you wish," she says.

Maybe I should be wishing for a long life. Maybe I should try and think of myself as old and happy, but I can't. All I can think of is Andy sitting outside this room and what it would feel like to kiss him tonight. So I think on that as she holds my hands, and when she lets go and tells me I can open them again, I'm sorry I'm not thinking of that kiss anymore. She stares at me. I want to ask her if my wish will come true, but she looks at me with sad eyes. She says, "Some wishes are meant to come true. Others are not. You will be fine." This sends such a wave of disappointment through me. I wish I hadn't agreed to do this. I think this is my cue to get up. I do and she says, "Send in . . . your boyfriend?" she asks.

I shake my head, "He's just a friend." So much for being a psychic.

"Oh," she says. "That's . . . good." I nod and thank her, though I don't know why since she just told me my life is going to suck.

I go through the curtain and spot Andy. "Your turn." I tell him.

"How was it?" he asks.

"Weird," I say.

Fifteen minutes later, and he's still not out. I wonder if I took this long. My reading only felt like two minutes. Probably because I am going to die young and the poor woman had to make some stuff up on the spot. After all, a psychic wouldn't tell you you're going to die soon, would she? But if that's what she saw, a warning would have been nice.

A few minutes later, Andy comes out.

"So," I ask, "what'd she say to you?" The psychic walks out behind him with a strange expression on her face.

"You really want to know?" he asks as we head outside.

"Of course."

"She said I'm going to die tomorrow," he says.

"Yeah, right. Me, too," I say and laugh.

The sound of wind chimes cuts through my laughter, and when I look back I see the old woman standing by the door, looking down the street at us.

"Remember," she calls. "You can make your own future." She points one crooked finger at Andy.

Andy stares at her and then turns away. "Scam," he says to me.

Chapter 20

TONIGHT

Colin and I head inside. The smell of the store and the sound of the chimes instantly take me back to my night with Andy.

But the woman who comes out from behind the curtain is not the same one from the previous night. This one is much younger, with short black hair.

"Can I help you guys?" she asks.

Colin looks at me and waits.

"I, uh . . ." They both stare at me expectantly. "I was looking for the lady, with the long hair." Colin raises an eyebrow but doesn't say anything.

"Oh, that's my mother," the young woman explains. "We both work here. She's not here tonight, but I can help you. Would you like a reading?"

Colin looks semiamused, until I say, "No . . . but he does."

"Me?" Colin says.

"Yes, you," I say. "Twenty dollars right?" I ask.

"For a psychic reading, yes," says the lady.

Colin says, "Frenchie, I don't want a reading."

"Yes, you do," I tell him. "Please." Even I can hear the desperation in my voice. I clear my throat. "Please," I say again.

He holds my gaze for a minute and then says, "Fine, but you have to get one too."

I nod, even though I'm not sure if I will and besides, I'm kind of broke now. "You first," I say.

Colin takes a twenty out of his wallet and says, "I can't believe you're asking me to do this," as he hands it to the woman.

She takes the twenty and tucks it away in the register before going to the door and flipping the sign to CLOSED. And then Colin and the psychic disappear to the back room.

And here I am, like Andy was that night. What would he have been thinking? I walk around the store, wondering what things Andy paid attention to while he was out here and I was back there with the other woman.

Did he know yet he would go through with it? Was he looking at everything like it was the last time he would see it?

There are healing crystals, tarot cards, incense burners, books on palm and tarot reading, and little sculptures of moons and hearts and gargoyles. I pick up a book about gargoyles and read how they're supposed to scare away evil.

Did Andy read this? I wonder what he thought about all this New Age stuff. Did he believe in it? Was he looking for something to believe in that night? Did I let him down?

Maybe Andy and I shouldn't have come here. Things might have been different if he hadn't run into me. If the old woman hadn't given him a doomish future. Maybe she confirmed that dying young was his destiny. Is that why we came here? In this tiny shop on Orange Avenue, did Andy really expect to find his destiny here? Or was this just the beginning of a cause and effect, like dominoes. And once we set that first domino into motion, there was nothing to stop all the rest from falling.

Colin comes out from behind the curtain and I can hear him thanking the woman. I head back to the front of the store.

"Your turn," he says.

"No, I don't . . ."

"Come on. You made me do it, so now it's your turn."

"Fine," I say and take out my wallet to use the emergency credit card my parents make me carry. I can only imagine what Mom will think when she sees the statement with this psychic shop listed on it.

But just then, the woman stares at me and says suddenly, "Put that away. Come with me."

Before I can refuse, she's already heading toward the back room and I feel like I have no choice but to follow. I sigh and head to the reading room.

We sit down, and I find myself just as fidgety and unsure as last time. Especially when she studies me and doesn't say anything or ask for my hand.

"Your aura . . . ," she says. Then she sits back and looks at me some more. I wait for her riddles.

"I'm not going to give you a reading," she finally says.

"Okay?"

"That's not why I brought you back here. A reading wouldn't be good for you," she says and shakes her head decidedly. "But you've been here before," she says. I swallow the lump in my throat. "That boy"—she says as she points her finger at the closed door and I know she's referring to Colin—"he's not the same one as before." She leans toward me. "There was another one." She's not asking me. She knows. "He's gone, isn't he?" she says.

I nod.

"My mother came home upset four months ago. She knew."

I feel like I've been punched in the stomach when she mentions this.

"And now, I'll tell you the only thing that matters. It's that you make your own future. People come here for answers, looking for something, looking for hope or promise. He came here looking for confirmation." She looks down and shakes her head again. "Confirmation is something we can never give you.

Warnings, perhaps, but never confirmation. I can't confirm anything. Because the future is like clay, every day you mold it, every day people leave impressions that change its form. It's never concrete, it's always changing. We might see some things, possibilities, but you are the one who decides what form your life takes."

I take a deep breath and try to wrap my mind around what she is telling me.

She sits back and looks at me. "What are you looking for?" she asks.

Answers. Andy. Myself.

I shrug.

"But if your mother saw, then . . ."

"She saw trouble. She warned him. He chose his own future," she finishes. I shake my head because I'm not sure I believe that.

"You will see," she says. "With time, you will see." And with that, she motions for me to leave.

I head out of the room and back to the store. Colin is flipping through some books. He notices me, but I'm already heading outside. I need some fresh air, even if it is stifling, humid air.

"What's the matter?" he asks as he follows me. I stand on the sidewalk, wondering what the hell I'm doing. The psychic's words stick with me but I feel like I missed something. Part of me wants to go back inside and demand to know what I should do, what I should have done.

I close my eyes. "I don't know. I just, I guess I was hoping for more of an answer."

Colin looks at me. "But you didn't want to get a reading," he says.

I nod. "I know." I run my hand through my hair in frustration. "This totally sucks."

"I'm sorry," Colin says.

We stand there a while longer, watching people head in and out of local bars and clubs.

"So," I say finally. "What'd she say to you?" The question echoes in my ears.

Somewhere, I hear the echo of my laugh from that night, but when I look at Colin, the laughter is coming from his mouth. "Wouldn't you like to know," he says. "But I'm not telling."

"That's probably better," I say and start walking.

Colin follows next to me, saying something, but all I can think about is if the psychic is right.

I cut him off and face him. "Do you think we really make our own future?"

"Of course," he says without hesitation.

"How are you so sure?" I ask him, shaking my head. "I mean, don't you think that on some level there are these paths to your life, already mapped out, that you follow?"

He thinks about this for a minute. "I don't know, that just seems so final. I mean, I honestly think of life like this big wilderness. And maybe you're on this path, but I always think you have a choice. To stay on that path, or to venture out into the wilderness and make different paths."

"Oh . . ." is all I can say. His answer has made my head feel full.

Colin smiles. "I'm taking a philosophy class right now at the community college. Don't be too impressed. Every class is a discussion like this." Colin and I make our way down Orange Avenue and cut through rowdy crowds of half-drunk people downtown. There are homeless people slumped on the sides of the sidewalks, little dirty heaps that blend into the buildings. A tall girl in a shimmery gold top is walking toward us. She links arms with the guy next to her and is close to one of the dirty little heaps before she realizes it, and then just steps right over him—literally.

"What about him?" I ask Colin who has noticed the same thing. "And her? Do you think she is this wise person who chose all the right paths and he chose all the wrong ones?"

"I think that's the gray," Colin says. "Some paths are more available to some while they're more hidden from others." He looks back at the guy. "Some people get tired of fighting through to better paths; some people get lost."

I nod, having the image of a huge jungle in my head. Some people strolling on by, while others fighting like hell. And some just giving up.

I push the image out of my head and look at the buildings as we walk.

"Last question," I say. "If you knew you were going to die tonight, what would you notice about this?"

"What? About here, like downtown, you mean?" he asks, giving me a funny look.

"Yeah, sure. This, or anything, or everything," I say.

"Oh, well thanks for narrowing it down," Colin says, but he stops where he is. He turns slowly in place, looking at everything carefully. Then he looks up at the sky, then finally, back at me.

"Do I have to be honest?"

"Please," I say.

"I guess, at first, I would try to notice everything, take everything in, you know? But I'd probably realize that's impossible because there's always something I'd miss. So then I'd focus on one cool thing," he says and moves in closer to me.

"One cool thing?" I say. The hairs on the back of my neck prickle.

He nods. "Yeah, so when it happened, when I'd die, I could just think about this one cool thing. . . ."

I close my eyes and breathe in the humid air. "Right."

"Are you okay?" Colin asks.

"Yeah," I say and walk past Colin quickly. "Let's just go. We have to keep going."

I lead us to Black Chapel Tattoo just a few blocks down and go in without explaining anything to Colin. He follows behind me. There are a couple of people waiting around, looking at the various designs on the wall. Some, I think, working up the courage to get one, and others that are so tattooed, I wonder where else they could manage to put more.

On the wall there are a bunch of tattoo designs to choose from.

"Know which one you're going to get?" Colin asks me.

Chapter 21

THAT NIGHT

"Know which one you're going to get?" I ask Andy.

He walks the length of the wall. "None of these are right," he says. He looks disappointed.

"How about some stars?" I suggest.

"Nah..."

"Maybe you should think about it and come back another time," I say.

"No... I want to get it tonight. I have to get it tonight."

"But why?"

"Because..." And I'm not sure he's going to say more as he walks to another wall filled with images. I follow him. "It's gotta be about now," he says. He looks around like he's searching for something. "Because you know what, Frenchie? Now is really all that we've got, right? The past is done. The future... the future is just too..." He shakes his head and I kind of understand what he means.

"Too big?" I ask.

He shakes his head. "No. The future doesn't exist. The future never actually exists." I'm about to ask what he means by that when he cuts me off and says, "But these all suck."

He shakes his head in disgust, but then his eyes meet mine and there's something about the way he looks at me that makes me feel stripped. Like he can see too much of me. Like he can see that I've been in love with him since ninth grade. Even though I don't want to break the connection, I can't keep looking at him this way. I can't let him see what I don't want him to see. I laugh nervously and look at the wall again. A fairy with a wicked smile gives me the finger.

"It has to be about now," he says. I nod without looking back over at him. I can feel him staring at me and my face feels hot.

I concentrate on the pissed-off fairy.

A minute later, he's at the counter. I breathe easier without his eyes on me.

"You coming?" he asks when a woman starts leading him to one of the ink stations. I follow, but I'm confused, because I didn't realize he had made up his mind already.

A guy with a tattooed neck stands up, introduces himself as Kaz, and shakes Andy's hand. "What are we getting today?" he asks Andy. Kaz has an English accent and he seems like a contradicting mix of formality and antiestablishment.

Andy looks my way. "I just want a name, over here," he says, grabbing his right shoulder.

"Right, then. What name do you want?"

"Frenchie," Andy says without hesitation. He looks at me and grins.

My mouth drops open as I realize what he's doing. "Are you insane!" I yell. "You can't do that!"

Kaz looks back and forth between the two of us. "A bit of a shocker for the girlfriend, I see," he says.

"I'm not his girlfriend," I say, even though my stomach gets fluttery over the assumption.

"Oh, well," he says and sits there, looking between the two of us. "She's right, bloke. You'll probably regret it someday, especially if she's not your girl. Cool name though. What exactly does it imply?" He grins at me.

"It implies that my name is Frenchie," I say slowly and deliberately. I resist the urge to add "dumbass" to the end of my sentence.

He laughs. "Right, then"—he says and then looks over at Andy and says—"well what's it gonna be?"

"Andy, you can't do this. You really can't. A tattoo is forever."

"I promise you, I won't regret it. And nothing is forever, Frenchie."

"This is really stupid, not to mention . . ."

"Just do it," Andy says to Kaz.

"You're sure then?" Kaz asks. Andy nods and takes off his shirt. Seeing Andy there, his shoulders and his skin, makes me lose my ability to rationalize. I look away nervously because all I can do is imagine what his skin would feel like against my lips. And then, the thought of my name on his shoulder kind of thrills me.

I shake my head. "You're crazy, you know that? Some day you'll have to explain yourself to your wife."

"I will never have to explain myself to anyone," he says. Kaz pipes up and says, "Right on, bloke. So you want this name in what kind of lettering?"

Andy shrugs. "Whatever you think. I'll leave it up to chance."

"Ahhh, lettering left up to chance. Impossibly impulsive," Kaz jokes. "Well then, give me a minute and I'll be right back," he says. Andy nods and lays shirtless on the chair. I sit at a nearby chair wondering why the hell he would tattoo my name on his shoulder. My name. It seems ridiculous and stupid . . . and on some level, incredibly touching and lovely.

"I don't understand why you wouldn't want something more . . . ," I say. I look down because selfishly, I do want Andy to tattoo my name on his shoulder. Shamefully, it would thrill me even though I would scoff at any other guy doing the same for any other girl. "Don't you want to get something more meaningful?"

"It is, though," Andy says. He smiles and I think I'm going to melt into the floor. I sit next to him and watch as Kaz draws up the sketch of my name in the back.

When he comes back, Kaz sets my name on Andy's bare skin. He peels away the stencil to reveal a most beautiful sight. My chest fills with giddiness and I feel like I'm atop the Swiss Alps breathing the freshest air.

"That's going to look quite fucking right," Kaz says. "Take a look."

Andy cranes his neck to look into the mirror that Kaz holds up by his shoulder.

"Perfect, man," he says. Then he turns toward me and says, "What do you think?"

I think it is the most beautiful thing I've ever seen. It makes me want to ask Andy if he wouldn't mind never wearing a shirt again so everyone can see my name on his shoulder and understand what it means, even if I don't. All I can say, though, is, "But it's . . . permanent."

"Frenchie," he says, shaking his head from side to side and letting out a low chuckle. "Nothing is permanent." And the way he says it makes me suddenly feel foolish. And I just want us to leave, but the buzz of the gun has already started and all I can do is watch as Andy sits there, with his eyes closed, taking in the pain of the incessant needle.

Chapter 22

TONIGHT

"So?" Colin looks over my shoulder. "Please tell me you're not going to get that one," he says staring at the pissed-off fairy.

"No," I say, shaking my head.

"Well, which one then?"

I shrug.

"Maybe you should wait," he says.

"No, it has to be tonight." The words echo in my head. And I'm suddenly quite certain, irrationally certain, that if I close my eyes and just think hard enough, think back to that night and recall every detail, then maybe I can conjure up Andy and he'll be standing here next to me, and that night will never have happened. Or maybe I'll suddenly time travel back and be able to stop him. I concentrate harder, trying to conjure up the people that filled this place that day. The three annoying girls that were giggling about getting the same tattoo on their lower backs. The girl with blue hair that looked disgusted when she walked by them. The normal looking guy with white sneakers that was passed out on one of the chairs in the front. And Andy, standing here, looking at the wall.

If I concentrate, I can hear his voice. I can hear my voice.

What about this one?

It has to be about now. I rewind and replay that word.

Now. Again.

Now.

I think I hear something in it—something I didn't hear then. I thought it was impulsiveness, impatience, excitement. But maybe . . . that was desperation? Was Andy desperate that night? But for what?

"Frenchie?"

My eyes flutter open and the moment is over. The portal to then closes, and I'm stuck in now.

"You okay?" Colin asks.

"Yeah, I'm fine," I say. I bite my lip so I don't yell at him. So I don't blurt out, "You ruined it!" Because that's stupid. Thinking these things is stupid, and I wish I didn't believe them. I take a deep breath. "I just have to do this. Tonight," I say.

"Okay," he says and puts his hand on my shoulder. I don't even cringe or squirm. "Come on," I say and we walk over to the counter.

The girl at the counter asks to see my ID.

"Shit, I . . . left it at home," I say, suddenly realizing that not being eighteen presents a huge problem.

"Right," she says, "Well, come back when you have it then."

"Really? Come on. I've been here before." I know it won't help to get pissed, and I probably seem like a big joke to her because she's heard it all before. But the idea of not being able to do this gets me desperate and irrationally pissed. "You have to let me. . . ."

"I don't have to let you do anything, sweetheart," she says.

I see Kaz in the background and realize he's been watching the whole thing. He gets up and comes over.

"Hey, it's Frenchie," he says to me, and then turns to the girl behind the counter. "What's going on?"

"She doesn't have ID," the girl says, looking back at me like I'm some kind of trash.

"Darling, why didn't you bring your ID?" he says. Shit, now he's going to get in on the fun too.

"I forgot," I mumble.

"You come downtown without ID? Right. I'm buying that," the girl says.

"Well, I'll let it go, but Laurie here is a bit of a bitch, so you better bring ID from now on, okay?"

"Fuck off, Kaz," Laurie says. "You can't do that."

"Zip it, Laurie. I did her last one," he says. "Come on now," he says, gesturing for me to follow him.

"It's your ass," Laurie calls to him.

I sit down at his station, not sure if he actually believes I forgot my ID.

"Well, then. So you're getting one this time?" he asks.

I nod. "Yeah, uh . . . thank you," I say and look up at him.

He leans down. "She really is a royal bitch," he says. "So let's just say I've seen your ID, okay? Where you got that ID, well that's on you."

"Yeah, of course," I say.

"Let's get on with it, then," he says, "What are you getting?"

"I want what Andy got. In the same place," I tell him. He says he has a picture of it in his portfolio. He pulls out the picture from a huge drawer and says he just needs to stencil it real quick and he'll be right back. He leaves and Colin and I are alone.

"So . . . ," Colin says. I know he wants to ask me who Andy is, but he doesn't. "A tattoo," he says. "Pretty permanent."

"Not really," I say, "Nothing is permanent."

We get quiet for a while.

"Would you get a tattoo?" I ask him suddenly. "If you knew you weren't going to be in this life anymore, if you knew you weren't even going to be in your body one more day?" I ask.

He's looking at me differently, concerned, like he's figuring out bits and pieces of something.

"No." His voice trails off. "I don't think so, anyway. But . . ." He shrugs.

"What would be the point, right?"

"I don't know," he says, but I can tell he's thinking. "Maybe I would. Maybe for the experience? To know what it feels like?"

I close my eyes and lean back in the chair. "Maybe."

The next voice I hear is Kaz telling me to take my arm out of my sleeve so he can get to my shoulder. I feel strange partially taking off my shirt in front of two guys, even though Kaz looks disinterested and Colin has enough sense to look away or at least pretend to. I hold my shirt over myself as Kaz rubs alcohol on the area where the tattoo will go. He sets the stencil in place and pulls away the paper.

"Want to take a look?" he asks. "Make sure it's all right?"

"No," I tell him, because I don't want to look at it until it's done, until there's no turning back. "I'm sure it's fine. Just do it."

"All right, suit yourself. No complaining, then."

I nod and wait for him to go on.

"So," he says once he's settled and ready to start. "Where is this Andy fellow tonight?" I look at Kaz's reflection in the mirror at his station. He raises his eyebrows and smiles mischievously. I think he's having fun making what appears to him as an awkward situation even more awkward. I don't know if it's because he feels some kind of loyalty to Andy since he tattooed him that he brings him up. I look at Colin's reflection, but he's looking on as Kaz works so I can't see his face well or read what he's thinking. One of Kaz's gloved hands rests on my shoulder as the other prepares to shoot the prickly hot sting of his tattoo gun.

"Bet he's kind of pissed now." Kaz laughs. "But can't say you didn't warn the poor bastard." I know exactly what Kaz is thinking. "He'll probably come by and want me to turn it into something else. Ahhh, young love. Don't trust it," he says and points at me like he's giving me some kind of lesson. Then he begins. I grit my teeth, both from the pain and Kaz's comments.

"He's dead," I say.

The buzz of the gun stops for a minute. "Oh," he says. The buzzing starts again and for a while we sit in silence as he concentrates on his work. "My apologies . . . ," he says. He rubs at my shoulder with a paper towel. "That's really terrible. What happened?"

I close my eyes. "Drug overdose," I say and I have no idea why I'm telling Kaz this when I don't know him and Colin is here.

"Oh man. Are you all right?" Kaz asks. I don't know if he means because of Andy or the gun, but I nod regardless.

"Don't move," he says when I shift a little. "You know, I had a buddy. He went out like that," Kaz says. "It wasn't good. His roommate found him, drool and foam around his mouth. Says he probably was seizuring as the drugs took over. You never know how that shit's going to go. Hope the poor bloke went out peacefully."

The gun buzzes on. He starts dragging the needle, rubbing it into my skin, filling in the outline. I blink back tears because I'll be damned if I'm going to cry in front of Kaz and Colin.

I close my eyes, and try to focus only on the buzz and the pain, but all I can see is Andy. Andy in his room, alone, swallowing pills, lying down and convulsing to death. Is that how it went? Did he maybe change his mind halfway through it, but it was too late? He couldn't even get up to get help? Or was every agonizing second better than what he was leaving behind. I don't understand how he could've hung out with me all night and I didn't see it. I didn't see whatever fucking clues he was giving. Or I did, but I didn't know. . . . I didn't even know they were clues. We were just on an adventure. A stupid, shitty adventure.

I suck in my breath as Kaz rubs and scratches at my skin. I picture Andy here that night, the way I watched as my name formed on his shoulder. Was that why he did it? The experience? To feel a different kind of pain? A more bearable pain?

I picture him at the cemetery, his stiff body six feet under, my name on his shoulder, under all that dirt.

It scares me to think of his dead body. So I picture sitting next to Em's grave. I picture being in my spot under the tree, talking to Em. And one of her poems that I've read over and over again floats into my brain.

I like a look of Agony,
Because I know it's true—
Men do not sham Convulsion,
Nor simulate, a Throe—

The Eyes glaze once—and that is Death—
Impossible to feign
The Beads upon the Forehead
By homely Anguish strung.

"Almost done, love," Kaz says, and Emily's words are quickly replaced by the *bzzzzz* of the gun. I feel each prick of the needle, each burn. As I listen to the monotony of the buzzing gun, it seems to be reciting the words going round and round my head. I like a look of agony *bzzzzzzz* because I know it's true *bzzzzzzz* I like a look of agony *bzzzzzzz* because I know it's true. . . .

"Right, then. Have a look," Kaz says while wiping my shoulder and then holding up a handheld mirror so I can see it.

I'm afraid to look. I'm afraid that somehow my thoughts of Andy convulsing, seizing, foaming, lying stiff as a board at Greenwood have somehow morphed their way into the ink. What if I carry Andy with me that way forever?

"Take a look," Kaz says. I look up at the mirror.

My name is perfectly engraved on my skin, in black fancy cursive writing. The skin around it is red.

Just the way Andy's looked.

The more I stare at it, the less meaning it seems to hold. And I tell Kaz it's great and I love it, even as I realize that it could have been any name that night. It just happened to be mine.

"So he was your boyfriend," Colin says after we walk out of the tattoo parlor.

I shake my head. "No." I should say more so maybe he'll understand why I'm taking him to all these random places. "Just a guy I knew."

"Sounds like more than that."

I shrug because Andy was more, but he wasn't, and I find it impossible to explain that to Colin. Thankfully he doesn't push further.

"Where next?" he asks.

I touch the Saran Wrap that covers the tattoo on my shoulder. My parents will be thrilled. And by thrilled I mean totally pissed that I just marked myself with my own name for the rest of my life. Like there's some likelihood that I'll forget who I am.

The thought makes me stop. I know I have, but I haven't.

And the absurdity of that, of everything that is or isn't, suddenly hits me.

"Why am I even doing this?" I ask Colin. "I don't even know what I'm doing." I press down on my shoulder, even though it's sore as hell. "Something is seriously wrong with me. I mean, I don't know who Andy was, or who I am, or who I was, or what exactly I'm looking for, so why? Why the hell am I doing this?" I start laughing. "It's crazy, right?"

Colin looks at me. "It doesn't matter."

"What doesn't matter?" I say.

"That it's crazy or not crazy. Just do it."

"But . . . it's stupid."

"Whatever you want to call it. But do it. Stop looking for reasons or answers and just . . . let it be what it is. Something made you start this, whatever it is. Just finish it." He pauses. "So where next?" he says.

I don't answer. "Where next?" he repeats quietly.

"Lake Eola," I say.

"Let's go."

Chapter 23

THAT NIGHT

Andy looks at me. "Well, then, Frenchie, I guess we only have tonight. So where should we go next?"

I shrug. "Wherever," I say, still in awe from seeing my name emblazoned on his shoulder. "I still can't believe you did that," I say again.

"Why, don't you like it?"

"No. I mean, yes, I like it. It's just . . ."

"It's weird," he mumbles.

"What's weird?"

"It's just . . . I thought I would feel it more, you know? It actually didn't hurt. It's like I hardly felt it."

"That's good," I say.

He shrugs. "Anyway, where should we hit next?" he asks.

I look around. "Lake Eola?"

He smiles. "To the swans."

Lake Eola is a park in downtown Orlando built around a big

sinkhole that was filled with water and dubbed a lake. There's a big fountain in the center and swans everywhere you look. See, Lake Eola's "thing" is swans. There are live swans that hang around the park and big plastic swan boats that you can rent and pedal to the middle of the lake with someone as lame as you.

"Hey, want to hijack a swan?" Andy says. At first I misunderstand him and think he wants us to kidnap one of the real swans, which is actually done quite often. Why anyone would want to kidnap a swan, I have no idea. But every few years, you hear about a swan-napping on the news.

"Yeah, right," I say.

"Come on, it'll be fun. Nobody's even here." He heads over to the huge, plastic swan boats.

"Oh," I say, realizing what he means.

I see him go from swan to swan, all lined up in a row next to a small deck.

I look around. Nobody's really here, but I'm still worried about hijacking a swan.

"They're all locked up," Andy says, pulling at the metal chains and locks to see if by chance any are not secure.

"That sucks," I say, although I'm secretly relieved.

"Yeah," Andy says as he sits down on the deck. He takes out his flask and takes another swig. Then he takes out a new pack of cigarettes and offers me one. I take it and we light up.

I inhale deeply and let out a long plume of smoke. "I didn't know you smoked," I say.

"I don't," he says, taking a long drag and then coughing. I laugh as he recovers. "I bought these tonight because I just wanted to try it out. There's a certain appeal to the idea of smoking. I wish I could."

"What? Smoke?" I ask.

He nods.

"What's so hard about it?" I ask taking another drag.

"I don't know, it just tastes so bad," he says. "But I want to feel that way, you know? The way people look like they feel when they take a deep drag and it goes all through their body and suddenly they're relaxed and . . ." He looks at me. "Do it," he says.

I look at him funny. "What? Take a deep drag?"

"Yeah." He looks at me expectantly. I can feel myself getting flushed as his gaze settles on my lips. I feel self-conscious, suddenly sure they're chapped and peeling.

"Oh, come on," I say, rolling my eyes and turning away.

"No, I'm serious." He reaches out and touches my arm. "Come on," he says, "take a nice long drag and tell me how it feels." He keeps staring at me.

"Fine," I say, if only to get him to stop looking at me like this. I put the cigarette up to my parted lips and inhale.

And I know this doesn't make sense, because it is after all

toxins and poisons and whatever, but sometimes a deep drag off a cigarette is so good. Sometimes, that smoke floats through your whole body, through your arms and to the tips of your fingers, and the sweet goodness of it soothes every frazzled nerve ending. And when you exhale, it's like you're letting everything go. Like the smoke scoops up all your worries and expels them from your body and they're gone for that second.

"See," Andy says, "that looks good."

I open my eyes. "Yeah," I say. "It is, but the reward of that feeling doesn't come unless you put up with the total gross taste for a while."

"I know," he says.

"And it comes with a price, you know. I mean, I'll probably die a slow horrible death gasping for my last breaths through a pinhole-sized airway into my lungs that barely inflate." I stop and think about that for a minute. "God, that sounds awful," I say as I take another drag. "I should really quit. Besides, it's only the first drag that feels that good. The rest of this," I say, holding the cigarette up, "it's just not the same."

Andy takes out his flask and takes a sip.

"I think that tastes worse than the cigarettes," I say, motioning to his flask.

He shrugs. "Maybe. I barely notice anymore." His voice trails off. After a while, he says, "You know, it's not fair that they keep all these swans here. I mean, why? For our amusement and entertainment? Doesn't that seem kind of fucked up?"

I shrug. "I guess," I say. "But it's not like they're in cages or anything. I mean, they have a nice place, and the city takes care of them, and . . . it's not like they're in a fishbowl or anything. There's lots of room here and they wander around wherever they want."

"But it is a fishbowl," Andy says. "They don't have a choice."

I look at the swans on the lake. "They look happy enough, though. They don't even realize they're stuck."

"That's even worse," he says. I laugh, but Andy doesn't. In fact, he seems agitated by the swans' ignorance.

"But Andy," I say, "aren't we all being held captive in some way, shape, or form?" I follow it up with another long drag, half close my eyes and nod my head as if I've just said the most enlightening thing ever uttered. I expect Andy to laugh because I'm totally trying to lighten the mood, but instead he nods his head.

"Exactly," he says.

"I was joking," I say. "I mean, kind of."

"Hey, you know what these swans remind me of?" Andy asks.

"Hmm?" I say, flicking my cigarette butt into the water.

"The ducks in Central Park. You know, Holden Caulfield."

"Oh, shit, yes!" I say, and I didn't think it was possible, but I fall for Andy a little more in that precise moment.

"When he's all obsessed with where they go in the winter," Andy says. "Because the lake is frozen over."

I slap my hand down on the deck. "Yes! Yes! You're so right. Now that's a fucking good book."

"Yeah, it is," Andy says. He sighs and looks at the swans again. "But you know, at least those ducks go."

"What?"

"They go. They escape," he says. "Maybe Holden doesn't know where, but they do get to go. But these poor bastards, they're just fucking stuck here."

I look at the swans. "I guess . . ."

We watch them for a minute and I think he's going to suggest we kidnap all of them and save them. But instead he says, "If I were one of these swans, I'd run out into traffic instead of waddling around here the way everyone wants me to."

I laugh, but he just pulls out another cigarette and lights up. After the first drag, he shakes his head and throws it into the lake. "Damn," he says and looks up at the buildings around us. "This place is getting old."

"Yeah," I say, sensing that the night is over. That in a few minutes, we'll both go home and on Monday, we'll pass in the halls and maybe he'll forget tonight even happened. "I guess we should probably get going." I get up on my feet.

"Wait," Andy says, reaching up and holding on to my wrist. "Like going, going?"

I shrug, even though the thrill of more time with Andy awakens every cigarette-soothed nerve. "What else are we going to do?" The question strikes me as somewhat suggestive even though I didn't mean it to be.

"You ever been to the beach at night?" Andy says.

"Uh, no, but . . ." I look at my watch, realizing how late it is and a ride out to the beach won't be a short trip. "It's getting kind of late." It's past midnight already, and Cocoa is at least a thirty- or forty-minute drive. Plus hanging out there and then driving back will add on more time.

"Oh, come on. It's a Saturday. You have a curfew or something?"

"Well, sort of," I answer, feeling kind of stupid. Here I thought my parents were pretty all right for letting me stay out for shows even though it means I am obligated to repeatedly text them and I have to be home by one thirty.

"Come on, Frenchie. I'm going to die tomorrow, remember? You wouldn't want to deny me my last request. Besides, we're supposed to be on an adventure. It's our night of adventure!" He jumps up to his feet and takes another sip from his flask. His eyes are still glassy from the alcohol, but his excitement is catching.

I don't know what to do. I know I should go home, tell him we can hang out another day. But I do the math. It would take us thirty minutes to get to Cocoa, thirty minutes back. We'd be gone for maybe two hours.

"All right," I say.

"Great!" he says and smiles like I've just granted him a wish.

We head to my car, and when we're one block away from it, Andy takes off running down the street, yelling and laughing. I start running too and we're both running so fast that we actually run past my car which gets us both laughing even more.

"I don't think I've run like that since elementary school," Andy says, catching his breath.

"I don't think I've run like that ever," I say between gasps. My lungs are going to explode. The fresh air is too much for them to handle and I start choking on it, coughing like crazy. "Cigarettes," I croak to Andy through gasps, as way of explanation. This only makes him laugh again and it takes us a full five minutes before we both settle down and finally get in the car. As I turn the key, the Vinyls' song we were listening to on the way over here blasts back on.

"I love this song," Andy yells.

"You like them?" I turn it down a little so I can hear him.

"Yeah, why?"

"I don't know." I smile. "You just don't look like the type."

"The type?"

"You know. You're kind of," I look for a word to describe Andy—a category I can fit him into, but nothing immediately comes to mind. "I don't know," I say. "I just didn't peg you for this kind of music."

"Well there's a lot of things people wouldn't peg me for," he says. Another song comes on and Andy starts singing along, so I join in. Something about heading into the dark night, on mostly empty streets, with the music blaring, and singing with Andy Cooper, makes me feel incredibly giddy and full, and happy for this moment. Even though it doesn't feel real, I know it is. Andy takes out his flask and toasts the air before drinking whatever is left. Then he grows quiet and I realize he's fallen asleep. I wonder if maybe I should just turn around and head back. I wonder this through the next two songs, and then it seems dumb to turn back now, so I just keep going, heading to the ends of the earth with the Vinyls in the background and Andy Cooper asleep next to me.

The road to Cocoa is 520 and has parts where it becomes a two-lane highway with traffic going past each other in opposite directions fast as hell. The only separation between colliding head on is a bit of luck and a double yellow line. Cars and trucks speed past us and make my car shudder. With each pass, I think of how little it would take for a car to lose control, crash into us, and kill us. And while this scares me, somewhere, in the warpiest part of my brain, I think wouldn't it be something if Andy and I died together tonight.

When we get to the beach, I shake Andy awake. And when he opens his eyes and sees my face, he grins and says, "We're here?" and my heart soars with happiness at my decision not to turn back.

There's a breeze in the air with the damp scent of sand, salt, and seaweed. I breathe in deeply, realizing how long I've avoided the beach. But right now, with only the light from the almost half moon and the orange glow of the back lights of the hotels along A1A, it's perfect. It's actually nice, and the roar of the ocean is soothing, even though they crash in a violent way.

"I haven't been here in a long time," I confess to Andy as we sit down on the sand, not far from the incoming tide.

"I come here all the time."

"With?"

"By myself, mostly," he says. *Mostly.* That's what sticks with me and I can't help but wonder, even as I feel I don't really have a right to wonder, how many other girls Andy has brought to the beach. "At night," he says. "Like this." He looks out at the waves and then asks, "So, why don't you come here?"

I can't really see Andy's face. Just his profile, which I'm studying. His question kind of catches me off guard and I blurt out, "Oh, uh, I almost drowned here when I was ten, at this exact beach actually."

Andy stops making circles in the sand. "Really?"

I nod.

"What was it like?"

"Scary mostly," I say. "I got caught in a rip current. You know how they tell you to swim along the shoreline and not against the current? Well I didn't know that at the time. So I just kept trying to swim to shore. It seemed like forever, and I kept swallowing water while the waves kept crashing over me and pulling me out farther and farther." I look out at the ocean, watching the waves. It's so deceptive.

"Then this guy comes out from nowhere," I continue, "and just scoops me up like some kind of giant and he gets me to shore. When I felt the sand under my feet, I just started walking, and then running." The memory of that day flashes through my mind. "You know, the weird thing is, even now, I can see the brightness of that day. Man . . . it was so bright." I close my eyes and the sun and the sea and every image from that day flashes behind my eyelids. "And the red swim trunks the guy was wearing. With white lines on the side. I remember all of that, but I don't remember what he looked like. I think I looked up at him, but his face just looked like a shadow because of the sun. Or maybe I was going to pass out. I don't know. But anyway, when

I start running, he calls out to me, but I just kept running, and I never looked back at him."

I open my eyes. "Isn't that weird? That I remember every-thing, except the *actual* guy who saved me?" I ask Andy.

"Why'd you run?" he asks.

"I don't know. I guess I was scared. Or worried I'd get into trouble or something."

"Did your parents freak out?" he asks.

"Are you kidding? I didn't tell them. I never told anyone."

"Nobody?"

I shake my head. "Well, actually, now I've told you so . . . just you."

"That's kind of cool," he says. "Well, not that you almost died, I mean . . ."

"I know what you mean."

"Sorry," he says, but I laugh.

"I'm just messing with you," I say.

"Right," he says and smiles but then he gets serious. "So, did you see your life flash before your eyes?"

I think for a minute. "I don't think so. I remember thinking about my parents, but I don't remember seeing the movie of my life or anything. Maybe it's because I was only ten. Mostly I just remember sheer panic, swallowing so much water, and a weird kind of silence—like someone muted the whole thing. I didn't hear the waves, or other people, or anything, just this . . . quiet. And how the sun made everything shimmer whenever I came up for air."

"That's crazy," Andy says. "Maybe . . . maybe you didn't see your life because even though it was a close encounter, it wasn't the real thing. Know what I mean?"

"Yeah, maybe."

We sit silent for a while and I want to lie down and stare at the sky, but I don't.

"Drowning must suck," he says. "Not being able to breathe and all. It must take a while and seem like forever." He looks at the water for a minute and then goes back to drawing circles in the sand again. "Do you ever wish you knew how you were going to die?" he asks.

"No," I tell him. "Never. I think it'd kind of suck to know, don't you? Besides, if everyone knew then everybody would spend their lives avoiding whatever it is that kills them, like the ocean, or cars, or whatever. And then, nobody would ever die when they're supposed to and we'd become overpopulated and we'd all die of famine or some shit like that"—I say and then look at him but he's just staring at me—"forget it," I say.

"No, I totally understand. It's like, some stuff is just inescapable. The more you try to avoid, the more it comes after you."

I shrug my shoulders. I'm not sure if what Andy says is what I mean, but it's getting late so I just say, "I guess. We should probably head back, though."

"Yeah, I guess so," he says. "But first . . ." He looks out at the ocean, gets up, and starts walking toward the water.

"Where are you going?"

I watch as he starts running, and then throws himself into one of the waves.

Shit.

"You're fucking crazy!" I yell after him because the water has got to be freezing.

"You're insane!" I head closer to the water.

"Come on," he yells. I sort of want to, but I don't. I just stand there and watch him.

"Just try it!" he yells.

I take off my shoes and walk to the edge. The water laps onto my feet and I suck in my breath at how cold it is. No fucking way am I getting in that water. I look back at Andy and he seems too far away. I want to tell him to come back, but all I can see are his arms as he slices through the water and goes farther out.

"Andy!" I yell, because if a current pulls him out, I wouldn't know what to do. There's no one here to help. Just me. And even now, I can hardly see him because of the darkness.

A huge wave comes in, and I totally lose sight of him. I blink several times, trying to make out something.

"Andy!" I repeat. I can feel the tingle of panic turn into a full rush. I yell his name a few more times and stare at the water, waiting for his head to appear somewhere.

The water rushes to the shore. "Andy!" I yell louder this time, but he doesn't answer. The waves rush in and back out. In and back out. My eyes scan the surface, again and again, and I'm just at the point of panic that makes your heart feel like it's going to jump out of your throat, when suddenly I think I see him. But I'm not sure.

"Andy!" I call out, and for a stupid, irrational minute, I look around, somehow convinced that I can conjure up the man in the red trunks that saved my life when I was ten. I wonder how long I should wait here. Somewhere, I have already left and am home and haven't told anyone that I left Andy Cooper in the ocean. Somewhere else, I'm running up and down this beach screaming and yelling that my friend has drowned but nobody hears me. Somewhere else, still, I'm just standing here, staring at the sea. My heart beats faster.

And then I definitely see him, coming out of the water, like he just suddenly appeared there. I'm so relieved I think I could cry, but that quickly turns to anger.

"What the hell!" I say as he walks toward me.

"That was such a rush!" The water drips off of him. "Oh man, that was awesome."

"Well, thanks for the fucking heart attack," I say and start trudging through the sand to put on my shoes. I'm pissed, so I half shove them on and then start walking without waiting up for him. "You probably screwed up your tattoo."

"I don't know, but it stings like hell," he says. "Man . . ." I look back and he's stopped. He's looking out at the water, and for a second I think he's going to run out there again.

"Let's go," I urge.

"It's so dark out there, French," he says. "It's a weird kind of . . . I don't know. . . ." He's still breathing heavy from swimming. I stop. "I mean, I went out there and I held my breath, and I just, you know, let the water pull me wherever and, wow. It was kind of . . . beautiful," he says.

"Or fucking stupid," I say. "It's not like you could've drowned or anything. Now, can we go?"

He nods and starts walking again. When we get to the car and start the drive back, he says, "Hey, I really didn't mean to scare you."

"Don't worry about it," I say, somewhat fine now that I won't have to explain Andy's drowning to anyone.

"And I'm sorry I'm getting your car all wet."

"It's fine."

He smiles and says, "You know, I really don't think it would be too horrible to go out that way. I could've stayed out there forever." He leans over and switches on the music. And I'm about to tell him it's not like that, not the way he described it at all. But I don't because the music is too loud and he's looking out the window. So I keep driving, pressing my foot down on the gas, as I try to get away from the dark, vast, crashing ocean as fast as I can.

Chapter 24

TONIGHT

"This one is unlocked," I yell over to Colin.

"Frenchie, don't you think this is kind of crazy?" he asks. But I'm already taking the metal chain off this particular plastic swan. Something about this action, releasing it, even though it's not a real swan, makes me think of Andy and how maybe he would appreciate it in some way.

"We're going to get caught. And they take swan shit seriously here."

I look at him.

"Well, not literally. What I mean is . . ."

"I know, I know. Come on," I say. But Colin is just standing there, his hands in his pockets as he stares at me. "Well, are you going to help me?" I ask.

"Fine, get in," he says. I jump in and so does Colin. We sit down and start pedaling, slowly making our way around the lake. I try not to wonder what this would have been like with Andy. I try to ignore the sense of betrayal that I feel as I remember he wanted to do this.

"This is kind of hard," Colin says. I'm thinking the same thing. I always thought this was like some lame pastime for people who were all about showing the world how romantic they could be, but it's more of a workout.

"Are you out of breath?" Colin asks with a bemused look on his face.

"Shut up," I say, completely out of breath.

He starts laughing. "You're pathetic!" he yells.

"You're the one who just said this is hard!"

"I know, but I'm not the one gasping for air," he says.

"I'm hardly gasping. And shut up," I repeat.

"Fine." He's quiet for a few seconds before he says, "So, why are we out here? I never would have pegged you for a romantic. Not that I'm not flattered. But swans, Frenchie? Really, I'm touched."

"Don't be," I say. I stop pedaling for a moment and look over at Colin who still looks amused by all of this. "Do you feel sorry for these swans? I mean, do you think their lives suck?"

"Well, I wouldn't want to be a big plastic swan, if that's what you mean."

"I'm being serious."

He stops pedaling and leans his head back. I wonder if he's

thinking how in the hell he got stuck here, with me. Maybe he's mentally retracing his footsteps, back to the night we met, and second-guessing having ever acknowledged my existence because now he's here, in the middle of Lake Eola at whatever time, being asked a philosophical question about the happiness of swans.

"Those swans are fine, Frenchie. Their existence or happiness isn't compromised just because the city put them here. I mean, what's so bad about it? That the city actually cares about them? That if they get sick, there's some vet out there probably offering free service to them? What's so bad about that?"

"I don't know. But doesn't it still seem wrong on some level?"

"Maybe . . . or maybe sometimes what seems bad isn't really that bad . . . ," he says slowly, as if he's trying to make sense of his own thoughts as they come together in his head. "I mean, yes, okay, I know I talk about the gray a lot, and I get it, some things might be black or white, right or wrong. But most things aren't that definitive, right? Good and bad is like that, too, in the sense that everything can't always be good, there's always some bad. And everything can't always be bad, there's usually some trace of good, right? There's that balance in the world, that yin and yang.

"I mean, think about it. The very second one person dies in the world, another person is born," he says. I look out at the swans. "Maybe you want to see the bad here, the imprisonment of the swans," he says with dramatic flare, "but look, they're good.

They have a sweet deal here. And who knows, maybe, somehow, someday the existence of these swans in this very location will make a difference in someone's life. Sometimes things are what you make of them." He puts his feet back on the pedals and starts pedaling.

I start pedaling too, and think about what Colin has said.

He looks over at me. I give him a sincere smile. He's making more sense to me.

"Keep pedaling," I say. "We still have a couple of more places to go."

We leave Lake Eola and head to Cocoa Beach. I park where I parked last time, and head to the same part of the beach Andy and I went to that night.

"Tell me a secret," I say to Colin as we sit down on the sand.

"What?"

I turn to him. "What's the biggest secret you have? Tell me something you've never told anyone before."

He thinks for a minute. "Well . . . Okay, here's something. I was a real jerk to this kid one time, for no reason," he says. "His grandparents lived next door to us and he would come and visit during summers." He looks at me and stops, like he's not sure he wants to tell me more, but continues. "My mom used to make me play with him even though I didn't want to. He was a couple of years younger than me and annoying as hell. That kid could keep talking on and on and never shut up. So this one time, I told him I was going to teach him a cool wrestling move someday. And I was, even though I didn't know anything about wrestling except for what I saw on TV." He stops and takes a breath. "So one day he comes over and starts talking and talking as usual, and I tell him I'll teach him that move now. I pin him down and I can tell I'm hurting him, but I just put more of my weight on him. And then"—Colin says and shakes his head and starts digging a hole in the sand—"then, I have my arm against his neck and I can tell it's choking him. But I just keep it there."

I've been holding my breath. I remember to breathe and Colin goes on. "I don't know why I didn't move it."

"Oh my god," I say.

"I mean, I didn't hate the kid that much. I didn't hate him at all really, but there I was, cutting off his air. And I see his eyes, how he starts to panic. How his face is getting red, and then a deeper red. And I just kept my arm there." He shakes his head and goes back to digging the hole.

"Did you . . ." I can't even say it. And I wonder if Colin has killed this little kid. If he already did his time at juvie and now I'm sitting here at the beach with him at night, alone.

"No, no . . . Oh God. No, Frenchie," he says, shaking his head.

"I mean, I let him go. And when I did, and he started gasping for air, all I'm thinking is I almost killed him, I almost killed him. So I ran inside and left him in my backyard. I peeked out my window and saw him just sitting there. Then he gets up and yells, 'Thanks, Colin! See you tomorrow.' Can you believe it? That's what he said."

I sit there for a minute taking in the story.

"Why do you think you did that?"

He bites his lip and shakes his head. "I don't know. It was just a stupid thing to do. I don't think I'm a mean person, and I would never do anything like that again," he says. "But something about that haunts me. I mean, it makes me wonder if there's this inherently evil side of me. I was" —he stops and kind of laughs— "for a while I had this kind of weird anxiety that I was going to grow up and be a serial killer or something." I can tell he feels embarrassed to admit this, and somehow it makes me feel better.

"I can't believe I just told you that," he says. "I promise I'm not as fucked up as that makes me sound."

I smile. "I know," I say. "Thanks for telling me."

"I think about that kid a lot. I wonder where he is, or if he's still that nice. Or if he ended up getting bullied at school." He shrugs his shoulders, like he doesn't know what else to say. "Anyway," he says. "Your turn."

I think about telling Colin how I almost drowned, but I

already told Andy, so it doesn't count. Or does it since Andy now took that secret to his grave? But I know that's not the secret Colin wants me to tell him. I know he wants to hear about Andy.

"It's stupid," I say.

"Tell me anyway," he says.

I breathe in deeply before beginning with, "Andy was this guy. . . ." I hate that I'm starting out like this, how so many other girl stories do. "And I . . . I guess I liked him, and one day we spent this 'one cool night' together." I look at Colin, but he shifts his gaze to the ground. "Not like that. We . . . it was like this. We did what you and I are doing right now. But now he's dead. He killed himself. And it doesn't matter because we weren't even anything."

It's the most I've said about Andy to anyone. Saying it out loud makes me feel even more weird and embarrassed about the night Andy and I spent together. I don't even know what it means to me, and I'll never know what it meant to him.

"Frenchie . . ." Colin says my name with so much sympathy that I have to talk over him.

"And now I think a part of me hates him and a part of me still . . ." I can't say it.

"A part of you still loves him?"

I don't know if I can admit this to Colin, but he's already guessed it. "Maybe," I say finally. "But how can you love someone you barely know? It doesn't make sense."

"I don't think things like that have to make sense," he says.

I nod. And because it's the first time I feel like someone understands, I can't control the tears. I pull my knees up and wrap my arms around them, hiding my face in the little refuge this creates, and I cry as quietly as possible.

"It'll be okay, Frenchie," Colin says gently, putting a hand on my back, now shaking with my stifled sobbing. "I'm so sorry," he says.

I don't know how long we stay like this. But finally I look up, wipe my face, and look at the dark water.

"Is he . . . is he here? I mean, out there?" Colin asks motioning to the water.

"No," I say, but in a way Andy is here. In a way, he's always here. He's been hanging out with me for months, walking behind me, telling me that a book sucks when I pick it up at the bookstore, reading other headstones while I sit at Em's. If I squint, I can almost see him swimming back to shore.

"Frenchie?" Colin says. But I'm already up, walking toward the water. I hear Colin calling me, but I'm in to my knees, and then my waist before I know it. The water is cold, but not as cold as it was that night. And I'm terrified. There's a part of me that feels he's here. There's a part of me that thinks he's going to grab my ankles and drag me down into the ocean and never let go.

"What the hell are you doing?" Colin yells, and he's suddenly next to me, looking at me like I've just lost my mind.

"Hold my hand," I tell him.

"What?"

"Just hold my hand," I repeat. And he does.

I close my eyes, hold my breath, and sink into the water. The salt water seeps under the plastic covering my tattoo. I reach up as the plastic floats away, leaving my skin exposed to the salt. It burns and stings but I ignore it and stay under water.

Images of Andy jumping into the waves that night rush through my mind, followed by images of the man in the red trunks that saved my life so long ago. The brightness of the sun is still in my mind, even as I sense the darkness of the water around me. I let my body bend to the will of the waves, but they don't thrash me around. I let go of Colin's hand and wait, but still, the sea doesn't swallow me. Finally I come up to the surface, gasping for air.

"What are you doing?" Colin says.

"I wanted to see something . . . ." The truth is, telling someone that you want to know if the sea will finally claim you and what Andy felt that night doesn't make any sense.

"Man, you're really freaking me out," he says.

"Don't worry."

He looks skeptical. "Come on," he says holding on to my

hand tightly again and tugging me back to the shore. "Can we just go now?" he asks.

I look at the shore, certain that on some plane of time, in some nexus to the universe, Andy has walked out of the waves and is getting in my car.

"Yeah," I say. "Let's go."

Chapter 25

"Will you stop here for a minute? Please?" Andy asks suddenly as we pass the Wal-Mart. "Let's get some ice cream."

"There's a 7-Eleven up a little farther. . . ."

"No, no, here, please," he begs.

It means I have to make a U-turn in order to go back, which isn't a big deal, but neither is just going to the 7-Eleven. I turn back at the next opportunity.

"You're high maintenance," I say.

"I know, I'm sorry." And after a minute he says, "You know what, it's stupid. Forget it. We don't have to stop." But I've already turned back and I'm heading into the parking lot.

"It's not a big deal," I say, although I am worried about how late it is and every minute that ticks by makes me more and more anxious. I'm only a little late right now, but each stop makes the potential of my parents' fury grow exponentially.

I park and then look over at him, still shivering in his wet clothes. "You look like you're freezing," I say.

"I am," he says.

"I'll go in," I say.

"No, I can go," he says and gets out of the car before I can object. I turn off the ignition and follow him. As we're walking in, I see Zeena Fuller, Andy's ex-girlfriend, walk out dressed in her work uniform, which explains why Andy wanted to come here and not 7-Eleven.

Zeena notices Andy and me as we walk across the parking lot toward her. I watch as Andy brushes by her and then notice the way she turns her head just slightly to look at him as he continues walking.

He stops suddenly and looks back at Zeena, who continues walking to her car. He looks up at the sky like he's looking for some kind of answer, then back at Zeena who is unlocking her car door.

"I'll just be a minute. Is that cool?" he says.

"Yeah, sure," I say, although I wouldn't really classify this as cool. More like awkward or weird.

"Okay, thanks," he says and takes off running after her.

I watch him as he calls out for her. The way she looks up at the sound of her name and waits for him.

I turn and go inside. The year-round air-conditioning that

is practically mandatory in Florida gives me goose bumps. I head to the ice cream aisle, which is even colder, and look over all the flavors.

I pick coffee. I look at my watch. It's 1:35. I'm officially in a shit load of trouble. I suddenly realize that Andy doesn't have a car, and I'll either have to take him back downtown or drop him off at his house, which I'm not even sure where that is. Then I'll really be late and my parents will totally freak out. I sigh and do what I hate doing. I call them.

My mom answers in a sleepy but loud voice. "Hello?" she says quickly.

"Mom, it's me."

"What's wrong? Is everything okay?"

"Relax, Mom. I'm fine. I'm gonna be late is all."

She sighs. "Frenchie . . ."

"I know. I'm sorry," I flounder for an excuse, but a flat tire will only worry her more, and running out of gas will only prove to her that I'm irresponsible. "I just lost track of time. I'm really, really sorry."

There's another heavy sigh, followed by bits and pieces of a conversation with Dad. Frenchie, late, ssshhh, go back to sleep. "How long will you be?" she asks.

"Well . . ." I cringe. "I'm still downtown and have to drop Robyn off . . . and Joel . . . and his girlfriend," I say, thinking this will at least buy me as much time as possible.

"Jesus, French!" another loud sigh, "Fine. Just get home, but don't speed. Be careful. And don't pull this shit again," she says. My mom is very motherly and all, but she can curse like a sailor when she's pissed

"Okay," I say. "I am really sorry, Mom. At least I called, though, right?"

"Goodnight, Frenchie," she says and hangs up before I can say anything else.

I decide I can't stand around and wait for Andy, so I look at all the other flavors, trying to figure out what Andy would like, but I have no idea. For all I know, he could be allergic to peanuts. Vanilla is too plain. Strawberry is too girlie. Chocolate for a non-chocolate lover can be overwhelming. And everything else seems too personal. Maybe mint chocolate chip? I finally decide on vanilla fudge swirl.

I pay and head back outside where Zeena and Andy are still talking by her car. I get in my car and start it up. Andy notices me and then turns his head back to Zeena. For an awful minute, I think I might watch them kiss, but no. It looks like Zeena is upset and Andy just shakes his head and starts walking back toward my car. I look away and pretend I haven't been watching them. When Andy opens the door and gets in, I fling the pint of ice cream at him and say, "Hope you like this. I didn't know what you'd want."

He looks at the label and nods. "This is great, thanks."

"You okay?" I ask.

"Fine," he says, but he sighs like he's just lost something. I put the car in drive and pull out. I look in my rearview mirror and catch a glimpse of Zeena, still standing where she was, looking at my car as we drive away. She gets smaller and smaller, and still she just stands there.

Chapter 26

TONIGHT

I'm strolling down the ice cream aisle with Colin as he studies the pint-sized cartons.

"What are you having?" Colin asks. "No, wait. Let me guess. I'll pick a flavor for you and you pick one for me," he says and smiles.

Despite myself, I smile, too.

"Okay," I say, staring at the freezer. My eyes scan the rows and fall on the vanilla fudge swirl. I can't help but think of Andy.

Next to that is Ben & Jerry's Cherry Garcia. I figure I can't go wrong with that because it has a little of everything, so I open the freezer and grab it. Colin does the same on the other side of me.

"Okay, you first," he says, holding the ice cream behind his back.

"No, come on, it was your brilliant idea. You first."

"Fine," he reveals his choice dramatically. It's Cherries Jubilee.

"Well?" he says.

"I've never had Cherries Jubilee. It looks so . . . pink," I say.

"Don't knock it. It's really good. Anyway, I figured you'd probably get something like coffee, but you should try this." I make a face, really wishing he'd chosen coffee instead. "All right, your turn," he says.

I reveal my choice and a look I can't quite read flashes across his face.

"Relax, it was just a guess. You can get something else," I say.

He smiles. "No, it's just . . . my dad had a thing for the Grateful Dead. He always got Cherry Garcia, even though I know he didn't really like it all that much. He liked chocolate, but always got this for some reason. He . . . uh . . ." Colin looks at me and shrugs his shoulders awkwardly. "He died when I was a kid."

"Oh," I say. I wonder why Colin didn't tell me this at the beach, but then, it's pretty personal and I get why he wouldn't. "Grateful Dead was a kickass band," I say. It might be one of the worst responses ever to news of someone's death, but it's all I can come up with. "I'm sorry," I say quickly. I'm seriously a mental case.

He shrugs off my stupid response before putting the Cherries Jubilee back on the freezer shelf.

"What are you doing?" I ask.

"Getting you coffee."

"No, keep that one," I say gesturing to the carton he's just put back.

"You sure?"

"Yeah, I want to try it. It looks . . . fun."

"What's that supposed to mean?"

I shrug. "Just, come on," I say.

"Say please."

I roll my eyes. "No, just get it."

"Say pretty please."

"No, just get the damn Cherries Jubilee!"

"Say pretty please. With a cherry on top." He laughs. "Say it or I'm going to start singing."

"No, that's stupid." I wait. "Come on!"

"Say it!" he yells. I don't say it. "Fine, you asked for it." He takes a deep breath and starts singing.

"Stop! Come on, shut up!" I tell him, completely embarrassed. A stock boy looks around from the end of the aisle, stares at us, but then decides we're not worth his time.

His eyes are closed, but he's way into his performance and looks ridiculous. "Seriously, stop!" I urge, but he keeps going, getting louder. So I ditch him and walk to the next aisle. I can still hear him two aisles over and I don't know what to think of the fact that he actually seems to know all the words to this song. I can't help but laugh because he sounds pretty terrible. And I can't believe there's not a manager around to stop him. He comes to the end of the song and I decide it's safe to head back. But as soon as he spots me, he starts over again.

"Please!" I yell.

He sings louder.

"Pretty please!"

He grins for a second, but goes for the high note anyway.

"With a cherry on top!" I yell.

He stops singing. "Good enough," he says. "Let's go," and walks to the registers.

We get in the checkout line, and that's when I see Zeena. I really want to toss the ice cream aside and run out of the store before she spots me. Right now she's busy ringing up this lady who apparently does all of her grocery shopping at one in the morning. Zeena looks miserable as she throws the woman's frozen meals into the bags.

"Seventy-four dollars and sixty-three cents," Zeena says. The woman slides her card through the machine as Zeena picks at her nail polish and waits for the receipt to finish printing out. She gives it to the woman who grabs it and then leaves. Colin and I move up in line. After she scans the Cherry Garcia ice cream, she looks up and sees me. For a second, she looks scared.

"Oh . . . hey," she says. I wave. She scans the Cherries Jubilee.

"Eight fifty-six," she says.

Colin pays her with a ten. She gives him back the change and we leave.

We're almost out the door when I exhale and realize I'd been holding my breath since we were at the register.

"You know that girl?" Colin asks as he crumples the receipt.

"Kind of," I say. And then I hear "Frenchie?" I turn around. There's Zeena looking at me, hands crossed over her chest as if she's cold. "You're Frenchie, right? Your name is Frenchie?"

I nod as my stomach lurches. *Is that Frenchie? Is that girl's name Frenchie?*

She bites her lip. "Do you think . . . maybe we can talk for a second?" she asks.

"Uh, sure . . . ," I say. She looks over at Colin who stands there looking back and forth between us before he gets the hint.

"Wait for you in the car?" he asks me.

I nod and Colin goes out through the automatic doors, leaving Zeena and me alone.

She stands awkwardly in her khaki pants and blue Wal-Mart shirt. She uncrosses her arms, smooths her hair back, and tucks it behind her ears. She looks from the Redbox movie kiosk to the missing person fliers on a bulletin board, to the dirty floor, before crossing her arms across her chest again and finally making eye contact with me.

"I'm Zeena. I don't think we've ever really met before. . . ."

Her voice trails off.

"No, I know who you are," I offer.

She winces slightly, but then nods.

"Uh, right. Well . . . I know you were . . . hanging out with Andy that last night . . . ," she says. When she says his name, she looks at me carefully. This time I'm the one who winces because Zeena Fuller is the only person in the world who knows that, and her saying it out loud scares me.

I don't know how to answer her. I suddenly worry I'm being set up. The thought that Zeena might be wearing a wire and the police are staking out the place crosses my mind even though I know it's ridiculous. I didn't do anything illegal by hanging out with Andy that night. Even if the cops come charging in and throw me to the ground, I'll . . . but then I remember the pills in my pocket. Shit.

"It was you, right?"

I stare at her. I don't say anything. What does she mean it was me? Like it was me that killed him? It was me that didn't stop him? It was me who should have?

She waits and looks down at her olive green Toms shoes, the shoes that help people around the world. I look down at my own beat-up shoes. They look like hell.

"I'm sorry," she says and shakes her head like she's confused. "I thought—"

"It was me," I blurt out.

She sighs. I don't know if it means she's relieved or if that's the cue for officers to rush in. "Oh, okay. I thought so." She smiles nervously and I wonder if that's it. If that's all Zeena had to say to me because now she's the one standing there saying nothing. She's studying the Redbox kiosk next to me. "Those movies suck," she says. "We watched almost all of them."

I turn and look at the movies and I know she means Andy when she says "we."

"He'd come here every night, you know. Rent a movie and we'd watch it at my place because he said . . . he said being alone was sad." She says the last part so softly I barely catch it. "He always liked the most depressing ones." Zeena doesn't look at me when she says this, she just keeps looking at the kiosk. I watch her eyes scanning the titles. "Like ones about the Holocaust, or about some gross social injustice. Movies about things that made you sick or cry over 'mankind's capacity and capability for cruelty.'" She doesn't look at me and it seems like she's talking to herself. "He was always going on and on about our ability to be cruel, our disgrace. He'd even . . . he'd cry. I never knew what to do, how to handle that, you know?" she asks, like I might have the answer. "I mean, he'd sob and I'd just . . ." She shakes her head. "He could drag you down."

Zeena stands there, and I don't know what to say to her. She looks glued to that spot, looking down at the floor, unwilling or unable to move. For a moment, the image of Andy's mom, the way she sat there unmoving by his grave that night, flashes through my head.

"That last night," Zeena says, "he said to me, 'I'm going to be okay.' Out there." She looks out of the smudged automatic doors, to the parking lot, to that night. "Can you believe he came by to tell me that? And he looked happy and I thought maybe he was with you." She looks at me and I realize she must think Andy and I were more than what we were.

"We weren't—" I explain, but she interrupts.

"I was happy for him. I thought, good, because more than anything, I wanted Andy to be happy, but I didn't know. I didn't know what he meant. And it wasn't my fault," she says firmly. She watches my face and I can tell she's checking for my reaction. "I just need you to know that. I don't know what he told you, but . . ."

"No, I know," I say. "He never said anything."

"Not that there was anything to say. I mean it was what it was," she says. "I'm not even sure I know what it was." She looks at me again, like I might be able to tell her. I shake my head because I can't. "He wouldn't let anyone in," she says. "Not really. Not ever."

"I know," I say, not because I actually do know but just

because I'm not sure what else to say. But what I say makes a pained expression flutter across Zeena's face.

"I mean, not really," I say. "We never hung out before. Not until that night. I didn't really know him at all."

The revelation hangs there in the air with the smell of produce and lingering bleach. This somehow doesn't help and I suddenly worry that Zeena will interpret this as me and Andy having some kind of one-night stand.

"It wasn't anything more than just hanging out. I saw him at this show and he said he wanted to go on this"—I say with a shrug—"on this, adventure, and it was . . . I don't even know what or why we did it." I tell her trying to explain something I don't know how to explain.

"Oh," she says. "I'm sorry." And I wonder why Zeena is apologizing to me.

"Don't be," I say.

"I wish I could say it wasn't like him," she says, "but it's typical Andy."

Her tone makes it seem like she's knocking him somehow, which I don't think is fair since he's not even here to defend himself.

"Anyway, I just wanted to say that to you. I mean, he was great." She smiles, remembering. "He could be so great. But he could also get so weighed down with . . . life." She struggles to find words. "At first, I thought he was, I don't know, romantically tortured or something? I think that was what drew me to him." She looks at her hands and continues. "But that kind of person can be exhausting. They can drain you. Especially when he didn't want to be any other way. I don't think he liked it when you tried to show him anything different than what he saw or thought. He was just so . . . consumed." Her voice trails off.

I don't know what to think of what Zeena is saying to me. Somehow it doesn't match with the Andy I barely knew and somehow it seems to describe him so perfectly. It makes me more confused. Because this incessant part of me thinks, *Me!* I could have saved him. I should have saved him.

She rubs her arms like she's trying to warm them up. She takes a deep breath and lets it out. "Well," she says. "I don't know," and she shrugs.

"Yeah," I say. I feel like I should say more to her. Because I think I've been wanting to talk to Zeena for a while now too, but I didn't really know it until now. What is there to say though? Thanks? It's cool we have a dead guy in common? Now have a good life?

She turns and heads back toward the cashier lanes. But I can't leave. She's back at her register, leaning back against the counter, and looking out at the empty grocery store. I wonder if after all these nights Zeena has been here, working in an almost empty grocery store, if there's a part of her that always hopes he will show up with a movie from the Redbox. I walk over to her.

"Does he haunt you?"

And she doesn't even look confused. She doesn't even hesitate. She stares at me with her gray eyes and says, "All the time."

Chapter 27

THAT NIGHT

"Where are we going?" I ask Andy once we leave the Wal-Mart.

"I don't know," he says.

"I can drop you off at your house," I tell him.

He turns to look out the window. "That's it? Our night of adventure is done?"

I'm not sure what more he wants me to do. "I guess so," I say.

"But we haven't even had our ice cream," he says, as if he just suddenly remembered. He taps the pint of vanilla fudge swirl.

Mom's voice rings in my ear.

"I know," I say, and I'm not sure how to read Andy. I mean, here I was buying ice cream while he talked to his ex-girlfriend, but now he doesn't want our night to end. And honestly, I'm not sure I want it to end either. My mind races with a solution.

"Well, okay, listen," I say. "I was supposed to be home half an hour ago. But . . . let's stop by my house, I'll let my parents know

I'm back, and then sneak back out."

He smiles. "Really?"

"Really," I say.

He sits back and almost seems relieved. "Cool," he says. And while my plan sounds valid and simple enough to me, I've never snuck out of my house before and I have no clue if I can pull it off.

Five minutes later, I've parked in front of my house with instructions for Andy to meet me down the street. I quietly enter my house and go into my parents' bedroom to let Mom know I'm back.

"That was fast," she says over my dad's snoring. I remember how I'd told her I had to drop everyone off.

"Joel and his girlfriend got a ride home with someone else," I whisper. "I just dropped off Robyn on the way."

"Oh," she says, "Well, go to bed. I just want to get some sleep already."

"Okay. Goodnight, Mom," I say, "and sorry."

"Fine, fine," she mumbles as she turns over and settles in.

I head down the hall that leads to our kitchen, grab a couple of spoons, and put them in my pocket. Then I go to my bedroom and purposely close the door loudly so Mom knows I'm in my room. I slowly open my window and climb back outside. My stomach flip-flops as both my feet hit the grass and I slowly close the window. I stand there for a minute, waiting for the light in my bedroom to flick on and my mom to open my window and ask me what the fuck I think I'm doing. But nothing happens. A minute later, I'm heading down to the street to meet Andy.

Chapter 28

TONIGHT

"The cemetery?" Colin asks as I tell him where we are going next. We're already on my street when I tell him to drive past my house and keep going to Greenwood. He parks and I get out. The gates are closed, so we have to climb over the brick wall to get in.

"Holy shit," Colin mutters. I know he's thinking this is insane because that's what any normal person would think. But he scales the wall anyway, and pretty soon we're walking toward Em's grave.

"You're not part of a cult or something, are you?" he calls behind me. "This isn't like some kind of ploy for a human sacrifice, is it?"

After his little singing stunt, I'm kind of enjoying his irrationality, so I don't say anything.

"Frenchie?" he says. "Holy shit! What the hell was that?" And I know his foot has probably sunk a little into the soft earth. I don't know why the ground on this side of the cemetery is soft and mushy and I don't think I want to know. But if you don't know about it, it feels like you're sinking, and it's easy to imagine that the earth is going to crumble and the dead are going to rise up like zombies all around you.

"I just want to show you something is all," I say. And then we're at Em's grave and I point to her headstone.

"Emily Dickinson," he reads. "Wait, that isn't the real Emily Dickinson, is it?" he asks.

"No," I say, "This is a different one."

"Oh," he says, "that's pretty cool, I guess. And weird."

I plop down and eat some of my ice cream.

"I hang out here. A lot," I tell him through bites. "With her." I cock my head toward her grave.

"Well," he says, as he starts in on his Cherry Garcia. "Again, kind of weird," he shrugs. "You a big fan or something?"

"I guess. It's just that . . . I feel like she gets it, you know? Like I think things that sometimes might be weird to think, but then I read one of her poems and it's like she already understands."

"Like a song," he says. "One you connect with and you think the lyrics are genius but it's really just because it captures exactly how you think or feel."

"Yes, exactly," I say. "Like there's this one poem about a flower, right, but it's not. It's about death. And how some people see a flower and that's it. They just see a flower. But others see a flower and realize that while it's pretty and all, its head will soon be chopped off by the morning frost and the little flower is going to be dead."

"I'm guessing you fall into the latter group of people."

"I guess. You?"

"I don't know. I mean, I know the flower is going to die. But"—he says and starts stirring his ice cream—"I don't know." He shrugs. He takes a sip of his now ice cream soup.

I set mine aside.

"My dad," Colin says suddenly, "he almost died in front of me."

I don't know what to say, so I don't say anything. But it does-n't seem to matter. Colin continues.

"I think it was his pure will and stubbornness that bought him an extra week. He just refused to die in front of me. We were watching The Three Stooges one morning. My mom had an appoint-ment, so it was just us. He started laughing when Mo's hair flew off his head. But then his laughter turned to coughing, and more coughing, and then his face started getting red as the coughing became more violent." He pours the rest of his ice cream on the ground. I wait, wondering if he's going to go on or if I should change the subject.

"Then this white foam started spilling from his mouth,"

Colin says after a moment. "So I started crying and screaming as loud as I could. I don't know who I expected to hear me. I don't know who I expected to come and help us. But it was all I could do."

"Wow," I say.

"Yeah," he says. "He died a week later, in his sleep. It was a massive coronary. My mom told me later that he'd told her it was my screams that kept him from dying that day. Sometimes . . ." He stops and just shakes his head.

"Sometimes what?" I ask.

"Sometimes I think I should've been there the night he did die. I should've been there screaming."

"I'm so sorry," I say.

"I think about that. A lot. More than I want to," he says. "But when I think about my dad, I try really hard for that not to be the only thing I think about. Because"—he says with a sigh—"I can't let that be the only thing I remember about him."

Chapter 29

THAT NIGHT

"You live down the street from the cemetery," Andy tells me. He's waiting just a couple of houses down when I come around from the side of my house and meet up with him.

"Yeah, I kind of noticed that already," I say.

"Is it weird? I mean, you must see a lot of funerals."

"Yeah, but I'm kind of used to it. It's not really that weird anymore," I say. "I like visiting strangers' graves though. I don't know them, so it doesn't hurt." I pause. "You must think I'm a freak," I say, suddenly self-conscious of how I'm coming across to Andy.

"Not at all," he says. "Let's go down there."

"What? Right now? That's kind of creepy," I say.

"Says the girl who visits strangers' graves." He's already walking down the street without me, so I follow him.

Even though I hang out here more than I should, I've never

been to the cemetery at night. But I ignore the fear that's start-ing to crawl on my skin like a thousand baby spiders.

I follow Andy over the wall and into the cemetery.

"This is really creepy," he says, and I'm glad that he at least feels the same way. "But kind of cool in a weird way."

"Why did you want to come here?" I ask as we continue walking.

"I don't know," he says. "I've never been to a cemetery."

"Never?" I ask.

"Nope, never," he says.

"Well, I guess you're pretty lucky then," I say.

"Yeah, you could say that." Without realizing, I've led Andy over to my usual spot near Em's grave.

We sit down and Andy notices the marker. "Hey"—he says, pointing to it—"Emily Dickinson is buried here?"

"This Emily Dickinson is. But the famous one is in Amherst," I explain.

"Huh," he says. "Hey, remember that poem we read by her in Carter's class?" Mr. Carter was our junior-year English teacher. "The one about the fly buzzing when the person dies?"

I nod. I did remember the poem, especially the first stanza and what is in my opinion the best first line of a poem ever:

I heard a Fly buzz—when I died—
The Stillness in the Room
Was like the Stillness in the Air—
Between the Heaves of Storm—

"So you think that's what it's like?" Andy asks. "Like you're waiting for death to be this majestic wonderful thing, but then it's just like a fly? And even though you might expect all this white light or to see the face of God, or whatever, all you hear is a buzz?"

I think for a minute. "I don't know. Maybe. But that just . . . sucks. Maybe it's more like this moment of clarity, you know. I mean, we're here right? On earth, living. But obviously we don't know the reason we're here. And we don't understand the things that happen. But maybe when we die, that thing that blocks our understanding is removed and we finally understand everything, even the nonsensical stuff. Maybe for once, you get to see every-thing for what it really is."

"Where?"

"I don't know. Just somewhere, I guess. Somewhere better."

I look down to our empty cartons of ice cream and check the time.

"I forgot, I still have to drive you home, or is your car down-town? Do you want me to drive you there?"

"No, don't worry about it," Andy says, getting up. "I'll just walk."

"You're going to walk home at three o'clock in the morning?"

"Yeah, it's no big deal."

"It's no problem taking you," I say as we start to make our way past the graves to the entrance of the cemetery.

"I'd rather walk."

"Oh, thanks," I say.

"No, what I mean is, I like walking at night." We scale the brick wall and start walking to my house.

"Thanks, Frenchie," he says when we get to my house.

"For what?" I ask.

"For a really cool night."

I suddenly get a weird feeling, and for a second I wonder if Andy Cooper is going to kiss me.

"Andy, I can honestly say this was the strangest, coolest night I've ever had."

He nods and kind of smiles. "Me too." Then he looks down and says, "It sucks to be alone, even when you want to be." It seems so random, but I feel like I understand what he's saying. And I think I could talk to Andy forever, but he just smiles again and says, "Anyway, thanks again."

"Yeah, of course," I say.

He leans in, hugs me, and says, "You're a badass, Frenchie

Garcia," so softly into my ear that I feel his warm breath. It smells like liquor but I love everything about it, about this moment, and I wish he would just stay.

But most of all, I wish I had the nerve to say something more than "Rock on, Andy Cooper," but I don't. That's all I say.

He lets go of me and walks in the opposite direction of the cemetery. I watch him go and have the craziest desire to run after him and kiss him and tell him that this has actually been the best night of my whole life.

But I don't. So I just go inside, glancing back one last time as Andy disappears into the darkness. He turns around, waves good-bye, and I wave back. Then I go to bed, thinking about Andy Cooper. How I wish I had the nerve to kiss him. Hoping that I'll run into him at school on Monday.

Chapter 30

TONIGHT

"So this is where your night with Andy ended, then?" Colin asks as we sit at Em's grave. A few crickets chirp as the moon shines brightly over all the headstones.

"Pretty much."

He looks at me. "Then what?" he whispers.

PART 3

THE
MORNING
AFTER
WOE—

Chapter 31

I wake up the next morning, the night with Andy slowly coming back to me while I'm still half asleep. I feel the smile on my face as I recall every detail, every place we went. The image of his shoulder branded with my name.

I open my eyes. Did he really do that? What if he wakes up today and totally regrets it? What if he never makes eye contact with me again.

I imagine Andy in his room, in his bed. Maybe recalling last night the same way I am.

My phone buzzes and interrupts my thoughts. I ignore it, only to have it buzz again immediately after it stops. I grab it and see that it's Joel. He probably showed up last night after I'd already left with Andy and he's only calling now to give me shit. I debate whether I should answer it or not. It stops buzzing. And then it immediately starts again. What the hell? I decide to just answer it.

"What's up?" I say.

"Where have you been? I've been calling you," Joel says.

"Yeah. And?"

"French—"

"I was waiting for you last night," I say, cutting him off.

"French—"

"But when you didn't show—"

"French, stop. Listen."

"What?"

There's a moment of silence. Then I hear him let out a deep breath.

"What? Speak," I say.

"You know Andy Cooper, right?"

"Yeah, he was . . ."

"French, Andy Cooper is dead."

I'm sure I didn't hear him right. I know he said Andy's name because my stomach fluttered when he did. His face flashed through my mind, the way he looked last night. "But it's not just that," Joel says. "Andy . . . he committed suicide."

"What?" I don't understand what Joel is saying. "What?" I repeat.

"Gene Fitzer, he called Robyn. He lives two houses down from Andy. He said there was an ambulance and cops on their street this morning. He found out Andy overdosed on some pills."

"Oh my god."

"Andy's mom was screaming in the street when they took him away. Andy's dad had to . . . man, this is just so messed up." Joel stops and takes a breath. "He's dead, French. It's fucking crazy."

"French? You there?" Joel says when I don't respond.

"Yeah," I whisper.

"I'm at Harold's. Robyn and Gene are here. You should get over here. . . . Shit, French. I've gone to school with the kid since kindergarten," Joel says.

Silence.

Then, "I'll see you in a bit." There's a click.

"What?" I whisper into the receiver. And I know Joel hung up because there's no answer, but I can still hear his words. *He's dead, French. He's dead.*

At some point the phone isn't next to my ear anymore. I change into some jeans. Slowly, the words take on meaning. The back part of my brain that has been processing them pushes the information to the front part. I sit back down on my bed and shut my eyes, while those words churn around in my head.

Joel's wrong. It can't be real. I look at my phone. This is some kind of sick joke. They're confused. It was somebody else they wheeled out of Andy's house. He was down the street. Hours ago. He's somewhere . . . anywhere. But he's not dead; he's not on some gurney.

I frantically pull on some socks and then my shoes. I don't change my shirt. It's the one I was wearing last night.

Next thing I know, I'm outside. The sun is blinding. I stare at the sidewalk as I head to Harold's, I watch my black Converse sneakers pounding the sidewalk. Joel will be there. He'll tell me it was a mistake. Gene Fitzer will tell us he's an idiot asshole and got Andy's house confused with someone else's.

I quicken my pace, but it takes forever to get to Harold's. I feel like I'm walking in place. I feel unreal, like I'm in a movie.

Finally I see them ahead; Joel and Lily, Robyn and Gene, who we don't hang out with much but Robyn does sometimes. They're sitting outside of Harold's, up against the side brick wall. Joel watches me as I approach and stop in front of them. I wait for them to say something, to tell me it's not true. But Joel just takes out a cigarette, lights it up, and holds it out for me. I take it.

Robyn is leaning her head on Gene's shoulder. She looks up at me with red eyes, but doesn't get up. "Can you believe this?" she says.

None of them say anything else, and I'm afraid to ask what I have to ask. I take a deep drag.

"Are you guys sure," I finally get out. I look up at the sky because I can't look at them.

Gene says, "I saw it all go down this morning."

My knees feel weak, and I slide down onto the concrete, next to Joel. Gene recounts how the sirens woke him up, how everyone on the street came outside, how they watched Andy's mom fall apart, how Andy's dad had to hold her and drag her back inside. How Gene's mom was over there the rest of the morning and saw Andy's suicide note on the table. A lousy suicide note that consisted of four words.

Four words. No explanation. No apologies. No signature. Just four words:

"I love you. Bye."

All of this should be enough proof, but I can't help but think, *Did you see him? Did you check the body bag? Did you see if it was actually him?*

Gene keeps talking. His mouth is moving, but I don't know what he's saying anymore. I'm suddenly on a strange street watching it all happen. Watching them push the gurney out, stopping the paramedics, unzipping the bag.

And there's Andy Cooper. He opens his eyes and smiles. "You're a badass, Frenchie," he says.

I close my eyes, and when I open them again, I'm back at Harold's. I hear Gene's voice and Joel's and Lily's and Robyn's. I listen as the same things are repeated until they've all been said a number of different ways. And then we sit there in the silence that comes after everyone has nothing more to say. We sit under a burning sun and we sweat and we smoke. I take drag after drag, until we have no cigarettes left, until I feel dizzy and nauseated. And then I pull out from Joel's arm around my shoulder and I go home.

I go straight to my bathroom and throw up. I strip off all my clothes. I hold the T-shirt I was wearing last night in my hand, and hold it up to my face because maybe it will smell like Andy. But it just smells like cigarettes and makes me cry. So I turn the water on as hot as it will go. I sit in the shower, letting the water burn my back. I try to melt the words that are rushing through my head, the words that are exploding and falling like debris in my brain. The ones that I can't stop.

Chapter 32

After a death there are things like strange spontaneous gatherings and student-led prayers in the courtyard during lunch. There are moments of silence during morning announcements. There are girls who give out ribbons with Andy's name on them to everyone. And all these things make you want to hate everyone at your school more than you already do.

After these things, there's a wake. And almost everyone goes because you hear about it. It becomes the topic of lunchroom discussions until the funeral. And that's the big finale. That's what everyone is waiting for.

Andy's funeral is on a Wednesday. Instead I go to school and sit in my empty classes. I stare out the windows. It's the sunniest fucking day of the year, and I can barely see because of the brightness. At first I don't think much of it. But then it bothers me more as the day goes on, with its obnoxious brilliance and radiant disposition. There should be rolling gray clouds. There should be rain.

The substitute filling in for my economics teacher comes by my desk and gently whispers, "There are grief counselors on campus if you feel you need to talk to someone." I look over at a girl in the room who is actually using the free period to color. I can't take it anymore and grab my stuff and leave.

I had made this big thing about not going to Andy's funeral. It was a matter of principle, I thought. So I'm a little disgusted with myself when I park in my driveway, get out of the car, and walk to the cemetery. I don't want to be a hypocrite. I don't want to be the person who barely knew him but came to watch to either be a part of the crowd or fulfill some morbid curiosity.

But here I am, at Em's grave, waiting for Andy. Waiting for them all to file in after him.

"Andy Cooper is dead," I tell her. And then I repeat it because it sounds so strange. *Andy Cooper is dead.* The cars come in through the gates, the same gates we climbed four nights ago. And I think of how he knew. How even as we climbed those gates, he knew he might be among these graves in just a few days. I wonder what kind of person can do that. I wonder who the hell Andy really was.

They wind around the cemetery, around the paved trails. It's the longest trail of cars I've ever seen. It looks like a sick game of follow the leader. And then they get out, appropriately solemn.

The guys wear sunglasses. The girls walk together and cry or talk in whispers.

And then there's Zeena, standing at the gates by herself. She stares at the crowd. And then, as if she can't look at them anymore, she looks around at the trees in the cemetery. For a moment I think she sees me, but her gaze goes right past me. Just when I think she's going to walk in, she turns around and leaves. She can't handle the show either, and I admire her ability to go. Me, I have to sit here and watch it all.

"Is he with you?" I ask Em. Maybe now that he's dead, you'll know him better than all of us. Maybe now you know his secrets. And maybe, Em, maybe you'll tell me.

But she doesn't.

"What do you think they'll do next, Em? Plant trees at school?" And I somewhat laugh at that.

I watch everyone and can't help wondering that if I were to die tomorrow, would these same people show up to my funeral? I recognize their faces, I know their names, but I don't really know them and they don't really know me and I know they don't really know Andy. I wonder if there's a way I can leave Mom and Dad instructions for my funeral without totally freaking them out. Because I don't want these people at my funeral. I don't want them to make me into this idea of who they think I am, an illusion of being someone better than I really am. Because I'm not. And Andy wasn't either.

I know right now, they all love Andy. They are all recalling how awesome he was because of that one time he said hi to them. They'll tell his mom he was a great guy. They'll tell stories of the time Andy Cooper lent them lunch money. And they'll all think he's fantastic.

I want to tell them all to go home and forget about Andy Cooper. Pretend he never existed. And I want to tell them all that Andy Cooper sucked.

"That's wrong, isn't it, Em? You must think I'm screwed up to want to do that." I hug my knees to my chest so I don't do anything crazy.

I think that's his mom there, in the front row. She looks sedated. Maybe you become cold and still, like a statue, and never feel again after your son dies. I think she wishes everyone would leave. And I think maybe she hates all those people from our school because we're alive and Andy isn't. Maybe she's looking at them and secretly thinks, *Why couldn't it be you, or you?*

Did she see Andy's tattoo?

Any minute now she'll stand up and demand to know who the hell is Frenchie. Maybe she'll scream, "My son had 'Frenchie' tattooed on his shoulder. I want to know which one of you fuckers is Frenchie!" And then everyone will know how I just let Andy Cooper go home and kill himself.

Andy's mom will scream my name until they all look over here and point. "There she is," they'll say. "There's the girl who let him die."

But Andy's mom doesn't scream. And nobody points. Because they're all watching as he's lowered into the ground.

I should tell them it's all a mistake. Because if I don't, Andy Cooper is going to be stuck down there, trying to claw his way out.

But I can't get up. I won't. I just watch as they throw roses on his casket.

People start to walk away and they leave him there. In a few months, most of them will forget Andy.

And now the cars are leaving, a motley group of ants, filing out one by one by one.

I watch as a man, who must be Andy's dad, tries to get Andy's mom to leave. But she won't. And now, he's talking to other people who go to her as well. But still, she won't get up from the chair she's in.

He goes back to her. He leans down, whispers something in her ear, and then kisses her cheek and leaves.

She's the only one left.

Andy's mom stays there the rest of the day and into the evening. There are these guys in a white van parked near the grave. It's their job to fill the hole, to take down the tent, to collect the chairs. But they don't make her leave. They sit there for a while, leave, and then come back hours later and sit and wait some more.

They must know she's outwaiting the sun. We watch her, unmoving as the sun sinks down below the horizon. And then we watch as Andy's father comes back. We watch as she finally allows herself to be led away. We hear her cries; cries that instead of fading the farther she gets from Andy's grave, grow louder, until they abruptly stop and I realize she must be in the car. The only sound that's left is the steady sound of cars speeding on the expressway just outside the cemetery. And moments later, I'm almost certain I can hear the Coopers' car on that expressway, passing by, and Andy's mother still calling his name over and over from behind the passenger window.

And I realize that grief can't turn you into a cold piece of stone. But it can crumble you as if you had been.

The guys fill the hole, break down the tent, and collect the chairs.

I sit here a little longer. Even though I want to forget all about Andy Cooper. Even though I wish I were far away from here.

Chapter 33

TONIGHT

Colin sits next to me, pulling up blades of grass from the ground.

"Do you think," he says, holding up a single blade, "we're in this blade of grass?"

I shrug because I'm remembering that day, watching Andy's mom leave the cemetery. Although she's not here now, it feels like I'm still here, keeping vigil over Andy's grave.

"We must be, right?" Colin continues. "Well, they are. They're in this grass." He motions around to all the graves and then points directly at Em's. "Some part of Emily Dickinson is in this." He holds up the piece of grass again.

"She's been dead too long," I say. "The blade of grass Em was in is long gone," I say.

Colin becomes thoughtful. "Or it has disintegrated back into the earth, fertilized, and sprung up again. It's comforting in a way, if you think about it."

"Who cares," I say. I'm frustrated with his ramblings even though this conversation is right up my alley. I would normally wrap it around me like a blanket. But right now I can't get into another deep philosophical discussion.

"Oh, sorry," Colin says, "for wondering about death as we sit here, in a cemetery. In the middle of the night."

"I'm sorry, you're right," I say. "It's just . . . tonight, I thought I'd find something, or understand something, or feel . . ." I shake my head. "I don't know. Different, I guess. What am I not doing?"

Colin is quiet for a moment and then says. "Maybe it's not about doing what you've already done. Maybe it's doing what you haven't done."

"What do you mean?" I say.

He hesitates. "Maybe you should stop searching for him, for answers. Maybe what you really need to do is say good-bye," he says.

I feel like I've been punched in the throat. His answer is so obvious. So impossible and yet so simple.

"But there's so much to say. And I don't know how," I tell Colin.

"Maybe you'll figure it out once you start."

I set my eyes on Andy's grave. Going over there terrifies me.

"All you have to do is walk over there. That's all," Colin says.

Before I can change my mind, I get up. Colin does too.

"Maybe you should . . . I mean, you don't have to go with me," I tell him.

"You want me to leave?" he asks, sounding a little hurt.

"I'm really sorry," I say, "especially after dragging you everywhere tonight."

"No, I understand," he says. "I'll wait for you over by the gates."

I shake my head and look at the ground.

"Hold on, you want me to leave . . . leave?" he asks.

"I'm sorry," I say again. It's all I can say.

"Are you sure? I mean, do you really want to hang out here by yourself?" he asks looking around.

"Yeah, I'll be fine," I assure him, but he doesn't look convinced. I guess he figures that if I really were fine, we wouldn't be standing in a cemetery right now.

Colin runs his hand through his hair. "Fine," he says. We stand there awkwardly looking at each other. I feel I should thank him for doing this with me, but for some reason I don't know how to phrase it because a simple thank-you hardly seems like enough.

"Colin," I say, "I just want to say . . . this, tonight . . ." I have to stop myself. I don't know how to thank him without losing it.

He reaches for my hand and holds it in his. "I know, and

you're welcome." He squeezes my hand. "And you're going to be okay, Frenchie. I know it," he says before letting my hand go. He turns and walks toward the cemetery entrance.

"Colin," I say again. He turns around. "Really, thank you," I say. He gives a nod and waves faintly before turning away again. I watch him go, losing him in the shadows of the trees, until I see him scaling the wall. And then I start walking to Andy's grave.

There's an almost full moon tonight that lights up the whole cemetery. I find my way over to where Andy is buried, making out some of the names on the graves I pass. And then I get to Andrew James Cooper.

"Andy Cooper," I say. "I bet you didn't expect me to show up here. Or maybe you did. . . ."

I inhale slowly. Being here makes me feel exposed, like Andy knows everything. How I've always felt about him, and everything that's happened since he left. And I wonder how pathetic I must seem, after all these months, standing here in the middle of the night.

"There are some things I should tell you," I say. But the words don't magically appear the way I'd hoped they would. And maybe because they don't, I sit down and suddenly remember something. I take out the plastic bag of pills I got from Sid.

"Sid says hi," I tell Andy. I don't know why I remember this and I wish I could take it back because Sid shouldn't be mentioned ever again. "Forget I said that," I tell Andy. I take the pills out of the bag and hold them in my hand. I wonder what it would be like to take them all. To sit here and pop them in my mouth, to have them travel through my body. To have them make my heart go faster and faster, or maybe slower and slower.

"Did you take them all at once, Andy?" I whisper. "Or one by one."

They might kill me. Or make me end up in a hospital in a coma for who knows how long. Maybe he didn't really think they'd work. It's easy to forget what they can do when you see them, so small, almost pretty in your hand this way. And if you just take them, if you don't think about dying, it's almost easy to swallow them.

I try to imagine him that night. Did he sit and look at them and think, really think, about what he was doing? Did he take them with every hope they'd work? Or did he just pop them in his mouth, hoping beyond hope that he would live, even as he was trying to die.

"Was it that bad?" I ask him. I close my eyes and try to imagine what he might say, but all I can picture is his face from that night, his glassy eyes. So I sit here with the same questions I've wondered for the past four months. Why did our paths cross that night? Why out of all the people in the world, did Andy run into me that night? Why did he pick that night to go to that club alone? Why didn't he stay with Zeena instead of getting back into my car?

I close my eyes for a moment and let my mind wander as it gets lost in all the other ways this could have turned out. All the different versions of that night, of what was and wasn't and never would be. These are the kinds of thoughts you can only think of in the space between night and morning, between dark and light, between life and death, because they're too terrible or wonderful or stupid to think when the world is awake.

Somewhere, that night ends with a kiss. Somewhere, Andy Cooper is kissing me. Somewhere, he's waiting at my locker on Monday morning and every morning after that. Somewhere, we fall in love and I feel happy.

But then a muffled voice brings me back down to the ground. *Is that Frenchie? Is that girl's name Frenchie?* And the hard ground suddenly gives way and I'm falling deeper and deeper into the earth, so far that maybe nobody will ever find me.

I clutch the pills, checking if they're still in my hand. Is this what it would feel like to take them, to put them in my mouth and swallow them? Would it feel like I'm falling? Like I didn't even exist anymore?

Except, Andy does exist, I tell myself. He didn't stop anything. Instead he created more misery. Misery that got dumped on everyone who ever loved or cared or even just knew him.

Everyone who would have helped him if he'd just let them.

Tears burn my eyes.

After tonight I won't let myself think of any of this again. I will bury these thoughts as deep as Andy Cooper is now. And I will stop trying to make sense of something that could never make sense.

I clutch the pills tighter and tighter. I can hardly feel them anymore. I worry where they've gone, but my eyes are too heavy and I'm too tired to look for them. I think maybe I've crushed them. Maybe they've slipped through my fingers and seeped into the ground.

I see flashes of Em walking over to me in her white dress. She sits next to me. Her words fill my mind, fill tonight, until I can't see or hear them anymore. Until they dissolve. Until they become nothing.

Chapter 34

The ground under me feels cool and my clothes are damp on my skin. I'm tired and my eyes are too heavy to open, even as I become aware of the grass underneath me. Moments or hours later, a white brightness flickers behind my lids and I know it must be morning. The brightness hurts my eyes, but I open them anyway and sit up. My hands are achy from clutching the pills all night. I look at them and wonder how they ended up in my hand again.

I don't know if I was asleep, or if I died, or if I'm a ghost, because when you wake up in a cemetery, all seem likely somehow. But I do know that even as I lie on Andy's grave, even as his body lies just feet under mine, he seems oddly far away.

I become aware of the faint sound of cars swishing by on the expressway that sits on the other side of the fence. Slowly, they get louder, and then there's a jarring blare of a horn.

I jump up and leave the cemetery, urged by the worry that Mom and Dad will walk into my room any minute and wonder where the hell I am. As I walk, I feel like I'm in a dream. The sun, impossibly, seems brighter than usual as I head home. I'm sure that it's just fatigue making me feel slightly delirious. And maybe that's why, instead of climbing back in through my bedroom window, I walk onto the front stoop, unlock the front door, and go inside my house.

The aroma of coffee and cinnamon raisin toast immediately hits me as I walk into the kitchen. My mother is sitting at the table, my father has stopped midjourney between the counter and table, holding a mug of coffee in his hands. They both stare at me, with a mixture of disbelief and perplexity.

"Frenchie?" Mom says.

"Hi," I say.

"Frenchie . . . ," Mom says again, looking at my clothes. I can see how she takes them in. "Are you . . . just getting in?"

"Mom, I know how this seems . . ."

She's still looking at me confused. "It seems," she says slowly, "like you're just getting in." She turns to look at Dad.

"Are you?" he asks. They both stare at me, waiting for an answer.

I nod. "Yes, but . . ."

Mom shakes her head and gives me a hard look. "Unbelievable, French."

"Just listen, Mom, please."

Dad gives her the let's-be-rational-parents-before-you-tear-into-her look. I think he's thinking there's a possibility that maybe I was abducted last night and have escaped and run a hundred miles to safety.

Mom repositions herself. "You better have one hell of an excuse," she says, turning her whole body my way and crossing her arms.

"Okay," I say. "I'm just getting in because . . . ," I hesitate. I know there's no turning back. "Because I spent last night in the cemetery."

"What?" Mom asks. "The cemetery? Are you in a cult or something?"

"No, I'm not in a cult, Mom."

"Okay . . . ," Dad says calmly. "Then, please, explain why exactly you slept in a cemetery."

"Because that's where Andy Cooper was taken when he died. . . ."

Dad looks at Mom, who looks confused again. She says, "Is that the boy from school? Who died a few months ago?" I nod. "But I thought you didn't know him."

"I did," I confess. When Mom received the automated phone call from school informing her that a classmate had passed away and there would be grief counselors available to help students cope, she had stood there with the phone to her ear and said, "Frenchie, did you know a boy named Andy Cooper?"

She never would have guessed how my heart stopped. How I was sure it was Andy's mother who had tracked me down and was asking for me. Or the cops asking what I knew about Andy's last night.

She never would have guessed how hard it was to look unaffected when I said, "Andy who?"

"I'd known him since ninth grade, and I didn't tell you because"—I say while looking at my dirty shoes—"I really liked him. And the night he . . ." I find it hard to say exactly what he did but I force myself to. "The night he killed himself, we had hung out. And we had this great night. Or at least I thought it was great, you know, because we just talked and talked and he was . . . it was so nice. But I didn't know what he was going to do . . . and I was stupid because I thought he was hanging out with me because he liked me . . . but really, maybe he was just lonely or scared or"—I say with a shrug—"I was just there."

My mom and dad look at each other and then back at me. Mom has uncrossed her arms and sits forward in her chair with one hand over her mouth. Dad just continues to look at me. I can't read his face, but the look on it makes it necessary for me to direct my attention back to my shoes.

"Honey," Mom says.

"And then the next morning he was . . ."

"Frenchie," Mom says.

I wipe away tears. "So last night I went looking for something from that night, or maybe . . . him," I say. "And then I finally just ended up at the cemetery. And when I woke up this morning I was still there."

They look horrified and a little like they've already telepathically decided I need to see a shrink.

"Oh my god, French," Mom says, pulling her eyes away from Dad's.

"I know how it sounds. But I think I'm fine. I've just felt so . . . bad, and it just made sense, but I think I'm okay now. And I just wanted you to know."

I don't tell them about Sid or the pills that are now back in my pocket. I leave out Colin, the tattoo, and anything more because they're already looking at me like they need to start dialing numbers to therapists.

"I'm sorry," I say. But Mom gets up and hugs me.

"Stop," she says, shaking her head as she lets go of me. "Everything will be fine," she says. "You'll be fine. I promise." Then she lets out a deep breath and looks at my dad.

Chapter 35

After talking to Mom and Dad, I go lock myself in the bathroom and check out my tattoo that has been throbbing like crazy. It looks really red and I hope it's not infected. I remember Kaz's care instructions and resolve to do everything he said from this point on. But for now, I study it in the mirror and wonder if it can ever mean something different to me than it did last night. Maybe someday it will.

I reach into my pockets and pull out the bag of pills. I dump them in the toilet and watch them float around. I remember thinking last night how easy it would be to just swallow them all and I'm suddenly afraid of them. I flush them away, relieved to be rid of them.

I take a shower, careful to avoid my shoulder, and spend the rest of the morning sleeping. Mom comes in several times to check on me. She brings me cinnamon raisin toast and tea, as if I'm sick. I tell her I'm fine. But she hovers and then I catch her standing at the doorway, staring at me like I'm some kind of tragic case, so I decide to get up and get ready. For what, I'm not sure, but I don't want to lie around the house all day having Mom and Dad worry about me. I look at my phone and figure I'll call Colin. But I'm certain he woke up this morning absolutely convinced that I'm a freak. So I don't.

I consider calling Joel because I want to talk to someone. But things between us are so screwed up and I don't know how to fix them anymore.

So I dial Robyn. Even though I managed to piss her off last night too, she's the most forgiving. The phone rings in my ear and I wait, hoping she'll pick up.

"So," she answers. "I guess you're done having a meltdown."

I groan. I know I deserved that. "Robyn, I'm sorry," I say.

"Whatever. We're cool. But I must say, you were at your finest last night. Couldn't have done it better myself."

I cringe picturing last night. "I guess it was pretty bad."

"Like watching a train wreck," she says.

A sickening feeling washes over me as I remember all the things I said to Joel.

"But I get it," Robyn continues, "I mean, it's not like Joel has been the best of friends lately. But he's in love, French. Of course he's going to ditch us and act like an idiot."

I sigh, feeling defeated. "I know."

"And it's not like love is a bad thing."

"I know," I repeat.

"I don't think you do," she says.

"I do," I say. "Or I think I do. I don't know. It's confusing."

"What do you mean?"

"I don't know," I say, because I don't. And I don't know how or why I think of Colin when Robyn talks about being like that with someone.

"Frenchie," Robyn says like she's talking to a child. "What are you thinking?"

I sigh because I know Robyn is going to make more out of this than it really is, but I tell her about hanging out with Colin last night. Not all of it, just that we hung out and talked after the blowup with Joel.

"So wait, are you saying you like him?"

"I'm saying we hung out. And it was nice," I answer.

There's a long silence before she says simply and calmly, "Okay."

"Just okay? I thought you'd be screaming in my ear."

"Yep, just okay. Because I know if I tell you how happy this makes me and how I'm seriously going to stop being your friend if you don't act on it, you'll end up sabotaging everything." But her voice has gotten higher with each word, and I know it's taking some effort for her to contain herself.

I laugh. "Good," I say.

"Very good," she gushes.

"And thanks for, you know, not staying mad at me. You're an awesome friend. I love you, you know that?"

Robyn cracks up. "Oh, French! You're so cute sometimes. Listen, if it weren't for Bobby, I'd be all over you too, but alas. . . ."

"I'm not in love with you, dumbass."

"You are! You want me! You dream about me every night!"

I laugh. "I'm hanging up, now."

"Okay, okay. Just remember to cut Joel some slack. And be nice to Colin! Leave out your death fun facts when talking to him. And don't be so intense."

"Hanging up now!"

"And French, love you too, freak!" she yells as I hang up.

I hate to admit it, but talking with Robyn about Colin makes my stomach twinge with nervous excitement. It surprises me.

I go to the living room where my parents are pretending to watch a movie, even as we all know they're just keeping a close eye on me.

I sit down next to them, both as still as statues when I enter the room. I guess I've kind of freaked them out a little, and as they hold their breath and stare at me from the corners of their eyes, I wonder if there was any other way to go about it.

I feel bad for laying this on them like that. I'm guessing they didn't exactly have dreams of a daughter who would spend the night in cemeteries. Or a daughter who they believe can do something wonderful, but has no idea what the hell to do with her life.

Chapter 36

The only guy who's ever come over to my house is Joel. And one wonderful night, briefly, Andy Cooper stood in front of my house and I hoped he would kiss me. So you can imagine my surprise when, while I still sit with my parents watching some horrible infomercial that we've all gotten sucked into, a car stops in front of our house that I immediately recognize.

"Who's that?" Mom asks as she looks out the window and sees Colin getting out of his car.

"That? Oh, uh, just a friend," I say, getting up and stumbling over the ottoman.

"Joel?" Dad asks looking over at Mom. Mom shakes her head quickly.

"Let him in," Mom says.

"No, Mom," I say, "he's just . . ."

"A friend," she finishes. I notice the slightest hint of a smile in the corners of her mouth.

"Yes," I say. "And I'm not letting him in. He already thinks I'm enough of a freak without meeting you guys."

The doorbell rings, and I open the door.

Colin is in a fresh white T-shirt and jeans. His hair has been slicked back anew.

"What's up?" I say, stepping outside and closing the door behind me. "What are you doing here?"

"Now there's gratitude for you. You drag me around town all night long and not even a hello?"

I cringe a little at having my social disgraces pointed out this way. "Sorry. You're right. Hello," I say.

"Hello," he says. He's holding something behind his back. He brings his arm forward and casually reveals a red flower.

"For you," he says.

A rose. This is when a girl should graciously take the flower and coyly sniff it. Robyn's voice rings in my ears, and I try to be these things, but I'm not.

And so I just stand there, looking at it, and say nothing.

He shakes his head and laughs. Before I can say anything, he lets the flower fall to the ground and crushes it with his black sneaker.

"I'm sorry. I didn't mean to be like that," I say.

"Relax," he says, smiling wickedly. "I thought it'd be fun to see how you'd react."

"And?" I say.

"And you behaved quite Frenchie-esque. That is to say, horribly and exactly as I predicted."

"Well, thanks for that," I say as I salvage the few petals from the ground that didn't get crushed, and hold them in my hand. "I'm a jerk," I say.

"Actually," he says as he sits down on the top step. I sit down next to him and notice how soapy he smells. "I did bring you something." He digs into his pocket and pulls out a small button. The design on it is a black skull with red, pink, and green roses perched on the cranium. "I thought this would be more you," he says.

I admire the button. "This is cool," I say.

"Yeah, well I've always been into the whole Día de los Muertos art. I picked that up a while ago, but when I saw it on my dresser today, it reminded me of you." He shrugs. "Anyway, thought you might like it," he says.

I don't think I've ever held anything so perfectly me in my hand before, but I am now, and I'm touched and surprised at how happy this little button is making me.

"I love it," I say. "Thanks a lot."

He nods and wipes his palms on his jeans. "So, how'd you sleep?"

"Okay, I guess," I say.

"Do you get your best rest in cemeteries?" he asks.

I stop staring at the button in my palm and look at Colin. "How'd you know?"

"You didn't seriously think I was just going to leave you there by yourself all night?" he asks.

"You watched me?"

He looks down and I think he looks a little flustered as he rubs the back of his neck. I kind of enjoy his discomfort. "I was just making sure you were okay. I left once I saw you heading home." He looks at me, locking his eyes with mine, trying to read my reaction and I notice how his light brown eyes look brighter, almost hazel in this light, even though he apparently didn't get any sleep last night.

"Listen," he says. "I know you're probably all offended because you can take care of yourself and all that. But I was worried, so I hung around."

I nod because although my first reaction is to show how unappreciative I can be, I actually do appreciate it.

"Now if you please, I'm tired as hell and could use a quadruple shot of espresso . . . minus your lecture." He grins.

I can't help but smile. "All right," I say. "But just let me get some money."

"My treat," he says.

"No way, not after what I put you through. I owe you."

"Come on," he says.

"Okay, just give me a minute," I say. I get up and run to my room. And then I do the most unnatural thing I've ever done. I grab Em's book of poems from my night table and open it. I place the petals in it and close the book before heading back outside.

"I'll be back later," I tell my parents.

"Uh . . . French?" Mom says as I reach the front door.

"Yeah?" I turn and look at her.

She shakes her head. "Forget it. Just . . . have fun."

I nod and shut the door.

"Damn, you're stubborn," Colin says.

"I know," I say and start heading down the street toward Harold's, but Colin stops me and says, "No, no. Get in the car."

"What? Why?"

"No questions allowed. Just get in. Today I take you on an adventure."

"Last night wasn't adventurous enough for you?"

"No, not really," he says. "Just get in." And he holds the car door open for me.

I get in his car and he shuts the door and runs around to his side. He looks over at me and flashes me a smile as he starts the car. I'm nervous and weirded out, and part of me feels like running out of the car and going back into my dark room. But I don't. More of me wants to stay and see what happens next.

"You ready?" he asks.

"Yeah," I say. "I think so."

He makes a U-turn and heads down the street, in the opposite direction of the cemetery.

We go to a French café in Winter Park. It has the best croissants I've ever had and a cappuccino so foamy and sweet that I wonder why I've never thought to order something like it before.

"Do you like it?" Colin asks.

"I do. This place is great," I say.

He nods. Then he sighs.

"Listen, I know you're dealing with stuff," he says. "I don't want you to think I'm this insensitive prick or anything. I mean, I know . . . or, I don't know, but I understand."

"I know you do," I say.

Now I feel nervous and somewhat humiliated. Here in the light, away from the cover of last night's darkness, I feel oddly exposed. It's hard for me not to keep looking away from him. He knows all about these last few months, how I've been feeling, and all about Andy—things no one else knows. As I got caught up in the blurred line between two nights, it had all made sense; me chasing a ghost and crying in front of Colin and inexplicably plunging into a deep, dark ocean. But today is different. Today is not last night, and I'm not sure who Colin and I are outside it.

"It's just that last night seems so . . ." I can't explain it.

Colin watches me and nods.

"I mean, did it even happen? In some ways, it doesn't even seem like that was me. You know?"

"Right, like we were watching it happen."

"Exactly! So, it's just funny now, being here with you."

"And you," he says. He looks at me and I look away and kind of laugh.

"We sound like idiots," I say.

He smiles. "Maybe. But, I hope we can do this more?" he asks. I like the way his voice goes up at the end of that sentence. And I like the idea of getting to know Colin outside of last night.

"Yes. I think so," I say and smile.

"Cool," he says. He laughs, which I'm beginning to realize is his nervous laughter.

Chapter 37

Joel has ignored my calls and messages, which has me thinking on some level that maybe Joel doesn't really care about me anymore. Maybe he never did. And even though I want things to be good between us again, the more he ignores my calls, the less apologetic I feel. I keep telling myself to be the bigger person, but being the bigger person totally sucks.

"Wanna go to Blue Room tonight?" I ask Colin on the phone a couple of days later.

"Blue Room is eighteen and up. Besides, I thought you wanted to see that movie," he says, since I still hadn't seen the zombie flick I'd been dying to see.

"Not tonight. Sugar is playing, all ages."

"Oh," Colin says. "Is that a good thing?"

"Well, I figure it's the only way I'll get to talk to Joel."

"So he doesn't know you're going?"

"Not exactly . . ."

"What's he gonna do if you show up?"

"Who knows. But whatever. I'm the one swallowing my pride, which is a lot more than I can say for him."

"Are you sure you're ready to talk to him?" Colin warns.

"I don't know. But I'm tired of this, so I'm going."

"All right, I'll pick you up around ten?"

"No, I can just meet you there."

"Yeah, okay. I'll be at your house at ten."

"I said . . ."

"See you then." He hangs up before I can say anything else.

That night, Mom finds it necessary to say to me as I leave, "Don't spend the night at the cemetery." Dad agrees with a slight nod and raised eyebrows.

"I won't," I say as I grab my keys. "And if Colin shows up, tell him I—" But just then, Colin's car rolls up in front of my house. "Forget it," I call to my parents. "I'm riding with Colin!" Damn him, I think, even though I'm slightly impressed and a bit flattered. Which consequently makes me a little nauseated, but there you have it.

"Why are you avoiding the inevitable?" Colin asks as I get in his car.

"What's that?" I ask him.

"Don't act like you don't know." He smiles and I look out the window, not letting him see the smile on my face. I almost forget that I'm heading out to another confrontation with Joel.

We pull into the parking lot. When we start walking toward Blue Room, Colin grabs my hand. I'm waiting for him to just give it a squeeze and let go, but he holds on casually, as if it were the simplest thing in the world. Which in many ways, it is.

"Don't worry," he says. "It'll be fine." And I'm not sure if he's talking about holding my hand or seeing Joel, but either way, I think I sort of believe him.

The music in Blue Room makes its way down the street, and the bass gets stronger the closer we get to it. When we walk in, the music is so loud, we have to shout and lean into each other just to hear what the other is saying.

"Looks like they're setting up!" Colin yells.

Lily is onstage, looking spectacular as ever. She doesn't notice us, and I'm grateful because I kind of want to hide right now as I remember how spiteful and mean I was at her expense.

I nod and turn away before she can spot us. "I don't see Joel!" I yell.

Colin looks around, searching. I halfheartedly follow his gaze because now that I'm here, I wouldn't mind putting off this whole thing with Joel. But then Colin nods and says, "Over there!"

I look in the direction Colin gestured at and spot Joel. At the same time he notices us and acknowledges me with only the slightest nod of his head. If a nod could be cold, Joel's would take the prize.

"He's still pissed!" I yell to Colin. Okay, so I didn't exactly expect Joel to run over here and be grateful that I showed up, but what the hell? Did he have to act like such a baby? "Unbelievable," I say.

Colin shrugs his shoulders. "Really? It's so unbelievable to think that he's still pissed over all the crap you said the other night?"

My face flushes. "Forget it," I say. "Maybe we should just go."

Colin shakes his head. "No, maybe not just yet."

I look over at Joel who is heading toward the stage where Lily is. He doesn't even look at me again. I stand there like an idiot, knowing that he and Lily will probably just wonder how the hell I had the nerve to even show up here.

"All you can do is apologize," Colin shouts. "Don't try to prove your point! Just apologize!"

I give him a dirty look because how can I not prove my point. How can I not explain myself? The very idea is killing me and Colin can tell.

"That's not fair—"

He cuts me off. "Are you sorry?"

"I just..."

"I know," he says, and leans into me closer, his mouth right next to my ear. "But, are you sorry?" He pulls away and looks straight at me.

I think about it, take a deep breath, and begrudgingly nod my head.

He leans in again. "Then for now, just apologize. Explain later." His hand squeezes mine as I look back to Joel and Lily.

"This sucks," I say.

Colin shrugs his shoulders. "Just do it," he yells.

I take a deep breath and push my way through the crowd. I can see Joel and Lily laughing together, presumably at some inside joke, and while I'm still angry at them, I feel sheepish now for showing my face.

I almost turn back, except Joel has already made eye contact with me. And then I'm right in front of them. They stare at me expectantly as I stand there, suddenly struck mute.

"Hi, Frenchie," Lily says.

Of course she would be the one to try to break the ice.

"Uh, hi," I say.

"Francesca," Joel says. Francesca? Oh, that's too much.

"So you're talking to me?" I say.

He shrugs his shoulders. "Are you talking to me?" he asks.

"Does it seem like I'm not?" I can't help the edge in my voice. Lily looks between the two of us.

This is going wrong already.

"Can we talk?" I ask.

"Isn't that what we're doing?"

"Joel," Lily says and puts her hand on his arm.

"Fine," he says and heads toward the exit. Before I follow, Lily touches my shoulder and says "It's not really that he's pissed, Frenchie, he's just hurt."

I nod. "Thanks for the update," I say. Her face drops. I try again. "I mean, thanks, Lily. I appreciate it, really, I do." I don't know if that sounds any less sarcastic, but Lily smiles, so I take it as a pretty good sign.

I step outside and see Joel leaning against the building. He sees me, pulls out two cigarettes, hands one to me, and lights it for me. I take a drag and let it out slowly.

I search my brain for what to say. I try to think of something funny that will make him laugh, but then I remember what Colin said and just start out with, "I'm sorry, okay?"

"You're really something, you know that?" he asks.

"Thanks," I say with a smile, even though I know it's not a compliment.

"I'm serious," he says.

"I know. The other night was," I shake my head. "It was horrible. It sucked big time and I hate that it happened."

Joel nods, taking in another long drag. "Yeah, no shit."

"And I know I might have said some pretty terrible things . . . ," I continue.

He raises an eyebrow. "Might have?"

"Okay, I did," I say. "I've just sort of not been right the last few months."

"Really? I didn't notice," he says.

"You're not making this easy," I say. I stop and think of what I want to say next. I know Colin told me not to try and explain everything right now, but I can't help it. And yet, I can't quite find the words or get them in order.

So I start with, "Remember that night? The night I was supposed to hang out with you and Lily for the Tantrums' show?"

"That was forever ago, but yeah, what about it?" he says.

My mouth goes dry. "Well, do you also remember it was the night before Andy Cooper . . . died?"

"Yeah," Joel says slowly, looking at me.

"Well, I hung out with Andy that night. When you and Lily didn't show up. He was there and we went to all these places and it was such a great night. Or I thought it was. And then he went home, and I went home. But the next day you called and told me . . . and, I don't know, Joel. . . ." I shake my head because I don't think I can explain the rest anymore. I try to find the words, but he reaches over and holds my hand and we're both quiet.

Joel lets out a long plume of smoke. "Shit," he says finally. "Why didn't you tell me?"

I shrug and take a drag off my cigarette. "Because I just thought people would blame me," I say.

Joel stays quiet for a long time, and then he looks at me. "Do you?" he says.

"What?"

"Do you blame yourself?" he asks.

"I did."

"And now?"

I shake my head. "No. If I thought for a minute that's what he was going to do, I would have done something. I just . . . I had no idea."

Joel looks at the ground like he's ashamed. "And this whole time, all I did was care about what's going on with me . . . not even asking you what was wrong because I didn't want to face telling you that I didn't want to go to Chicago anymore," he says.

"You could have told me," I say.

"I know," he says. "You could have told me, too. Everything."

"I know. But it was too hard."

Joel nods.

"I'm sorry I didn't give Lily a chance. That wasn't fair and if I'd been straight with you from the beginning, I know you would've been there."

"I would have," he says.

"I know. And it's more than that, I mean, I miss . . ." I want to tell Joel I miss him, and our friendship, and how things used to be, but I don't want to make it seem like I hate Lily, so I don't.

"You know what I miss?" Joel says suddenly, filling up the silence. "I miss my dreads." And then we both start cracking up.

"But seriously," he says, running his hand over his baldness. "I mean, I like it, but I just cut them off, without really thinking about it. They were like a part of me, you know?"

I nod. I know what he's saying.

"It's a good change, though," I say. "It suits you."

"Thanks, but I still miss them." He looks at me. "And I'm sorry I cut them off."

I get the slightest bit teary-eyed.

"What, don't tell me you're going to cry," he teases. "Don't tell me the Great Frenchie Garcia is actually human?"

I smile. "Fuck off."

We laugh, and I'm grateful.

"So does your girlfriend totally hate me?" I ask.

Joel shrugs. "You know, I've never really seen her pissed. It was kind of cute." He smiles at what I can only assume is Lily looking like a pissed-off kitty. "But no, I don't think she hates you. She's pretty understanding. Maybe you should give her a chance."

"I will," I say, making a mental note to officially apologize to Lily. "And you? Do you hate me?"

"Only as much as you hate me."

"So we're good?"

"Always," he says.

Chapter 38

A few days after Joel and I make up, I sit on my front stoop looking across the street at the old man's house. There's a FOR SALE sign in the front yard and I wonder who will move in. I wonder if they'll know someone died in there.

I decide to get up and head to the cemetery.

I check my back pocket, feeling for the folded-up paper that I've already checked for several times. It's still there. I don't know why this is a big deal.

"Hi, again," I say when I get to Andy's grave. "I know I wasn't going to come back here, but I just wanted to say a few things I forgot to say.

"First, I'll always be sorry that I didn't save you. I feel like I should have done something that night, that somehow I could have made things different. And I'm sorry if I missed something that you were trying to tell me. But I can't keep going back to that night, because I'm in today. And I hope that tomorrow I'll be in tomorrow, because it does exist, Andy. It does.

"And second, I wanted to give this to you." I take out the folded paper in my pocket and read it aloud:

"'Andy Cooper was not a seeker of truth. He was a boy, like most, who woke up in the morning every day and went to school. He sat in class with others like him, and at the end of the day he went home just the same. He often looked at the world and tried to find meaning in it the way most of us have done or will do at some point in our lives. Andy Cooper probably wanted to be happy, like most of us do. He just didn't know how.

"'So on one lonely humid night in February, Andy Cooper said good-bye to the world, in his own way. That night he brought along a girl, which consequently changed her life. And then, tragically, he went home and ended his.

"'He is missed by his family, friends, and even those who didn't know him. And the future of many will be different because Andy Cooper won't be in it anymore.

"'He could have had a magnificent life. Or a miserable life. Or a quiet life. Many wonderful things could have happened to him, as well as many bad things. But in the end, his life was hardly lived. And that's what is most tragic of all.'

"That's it," I tell him when I'm finished reading. "See, you doing this, Andy, it didn't change anything. It didn't stop whatever you thought was so corrupt and horrible in the world. And there is a lot of horrible and corrupt shit out there, Andy. I get that. But there's also a lot of good. I just wish you could've seen that. I wish you could've lived and been able to experience that."

I look around the cemetery. I'm the only one here, and I'm thankful since I don't want anyone to witness what I do next.

"Anyway, last thing, and don't get pissed or haunt me or anything," I say as I start pulling up a patch of grass on Andy's grave and dig a small hole.

I want to leave these words with Andy. I don't want them to blow away in the wind or be washed away with the rain. I want them to become part of the very earth that will someday be a part of these trees, these leaves, and the world again. Like Andy.

My heart beats faster with each discreet scoop.

Once there's a small pocket, I quickly place the poem in there and start filling it up.

"Maybe you hung out with me that night because you were lonely. Maybe you thought that I was safe or I didn't care. I'll never really know. It took me a while to realize that but now I'm becoming okay with not knowing. But I want you to know that night did mean a lot to me and I did care. I do care. And I'll always wish you had known that."

I get up and pat down the earth with my shoe.

"Bye, Andy Cooper. I hope you have a good afterlife." I turn to leave.

As I go through the cemetery gates, a procession is making its way down my street. I keep walking, and soon the hearse is passing right next to me. For a brief moment, I pass right next to death. And something about it makes me think of how we pass people every day, how our lives do and don't intersect. How some lives end and others go on. And I'm grateful that I'm headed in the opposite direction of that corpse.

In the distance, I see Colin park in front of my house and get out of his car. He looks down the street and notices me heading his way. He stands there with his hands in his pockets, waiting for me.

"Hey," I say as I approach.

"Visiting Em?"

"In a way."

"You good?"

I nod. "Yep."

"Good." He reaches for my hand and we walk to my house. My hand in his like this, it feels like something is beginning, not ending.

"So, what now?" he asks once we reach my house and sit on my front stoop.

I shrug. "I don't know. I have to figure some stuff out. Like if I still want to go to art school. . . ."

"I didn't know you were into art," he says, and this somehow strikes me as funny.

I laugh. "Really? Yeah, I guess we haven't gotten around to that kind of stuff yet. But yeah, I draw and paint."

"That's really cool," he says, genuinely interested.

"Thanks," I say. "But I haven't thought about it or done much of it lately. I love it, but I just have to find that inspiration again. And figure out if it's what I really want. At least my parents are being pretty cool about it," I tell him.

I ended up talking to them about taking some time to figure out what I wanted to do, instead of rushing to reapply to art school. And they were surprisingly understanding. Now that I don't have any kind of plan of what I'm going to do next, I'm kind of excited about what it will be.

"Maybe I'll study something else, like writing or literature or something like that."

"Or both," he says.

"Or both," I agree, smiling at the possibility.

"So you'll be around while you figure it out?" he asks.

"For the time being," I say.

"And then?"

"I don't know. Maybe go somewhere else, see what's out there."

He's quiet and looks down at the ground, so I do too. There are ants scurrying around and I'm reminded of how I used to wish I were an ant whenever I had to do something I didn't feel like doing.

But then I thought of how they're always working and how someone can come by and unwittingly cave in their tunnels and destroy their world. But now I stare at them, thinking that in some ways, maybe they're even more evolved than we are. Because when someone does crush their walls in, they immediately start rebuilding.

I watch as Colin avoids crushing the ants.

"Which means," he says, "that I have just enough time to make you fall in love with me."

I laugh. "You're funny," I say.

Except he's not laughing. He's leaning back on the top step, smiling. "You know, I've always wanted to go somewhere else, too."

I raise an eyebrow and am about to offer a snarky reply, but he leans in closer and kisses me before I can say anything. When he pulls away he studies my face as if to ask if that was okay.

Having him this close to me, looking at me this way, makes my heart beat fast, but it's also comforting and makes me feel warm. And I feel like I could stay this way for a long time. I smile to let him know that, yes, this is okay. And then I remember something.

"What did the psychic say to you that night anyway?"

He pulls his eyes off mine for a moment and says, "Something about having the power to choose our own destinies." He looks at me again. "And recognizing when it chooses us."

"Do you believe that?" I ask. "That destiny can choose us?"

He reaches for my hand and turns it over to trace the lines on my palm. "Yeah," he says, "I do. But only the good things. And only if you let them." He continues tracing my hand with his finger.

I smile and watch him. It's not the answer I set out to find, but it's one I'm glad I did. And it is one I know I can live with.

If I should die,

And you should live

And time should gurgle on

And morn should beam

And noon should burn

As it has usual done

If Birds should build as early

And Bees as bustling go

One might depart at option

From enterprise below!

'Tis sweet to know that stocks will stand

When we with Daisies lie

That Commerce will continue

And Trades as briskly fly

It makes the parting tranquil

And keeps the soul serene

That gentlemen so sprightly

Conduct the pleasing scene!

Acknowledgments

Endless thanks to those who made this book possible:

Kerry Sparks at Levine Greenberg, for your continued enthusiasm, support, and advice. And especially for helping make the people who live in my head live in the heads of others.

Marlo Scrimizzi, for your insight, your brilliant suggestions, and thoughtful questions that made me think about this story in ways I missed and helped make it the story it always wanted to be.

Frances Soo Ping Chow, for an amazing cover and interior design.

Kate Forrestor, for your illustrations.

All my friends and family for their love, support, and inspiration, especially:

Mom, because I know you worried about me a lot and wondered if I was in a cult led by Robert Smith. I wasn't. I just really liked music. And the color black. Dad, because unknowingly, I asked you if I could go get ice cream the day grandpa died. You said yes and hid your tears. Nancy and David, because each of you may be slightly demented by association. Katherine, because you're strange and wonderful and you read this first. And Ava and Mateo, because each of you are *certainly* demented by association.

And Nando, always Nando, because you love me even though I'm slightly morbid. And because of so much more.

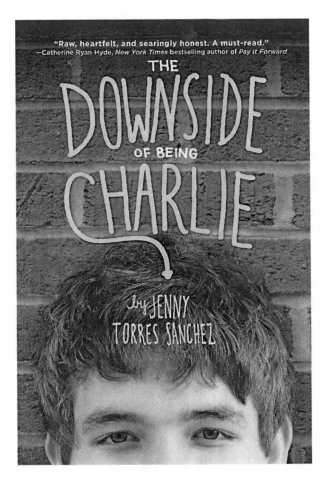

RP|TEENS

PHILADELPHIA · LONDON

CPSIA information can be obtained at www.ICGtesting.com
Printed in the USA
LVOW07s0847130915

453808LV00004B/12/P